VACATED LANDSCAPE

VACATED LANDSCAPE

JEAN LAHOUGUE

TRANSLATED BY K. E. GORMLEY

WAKEFIELD PRESS / CAMBRIDGE, MASSACHUSETTS

Wakefield Press, P.O. Box 425645, Cambridge, MA 02142

Originally published as *Non-lieu dans un paysage* in 1977.
© Éditions Gallimard, Paris, 1977.

Cover image: detail from François de Nomé, *Fuite en Égypte*, 1624.

This book was set in Garamond Premier Pro and Helvetica Neue Pro by Wakefield Press. Printed and bound by Sheridan Saline, Inc., in the United States of America.

ISBN: 978-1-939663-97-9

Available through D.A.P./Distributed Art Publishers
75 Broad Street, Suite 630
New York, New York 10004
Tel: (212) 627-1999
Fax: (212) 627-9484

10 9 8 7 6 5 4 3 2 1

To my mother

I

The singular case in which I was to become so deeply entangled doubtless began at my home on rue de H., street of mirror-makers and lamp-sellers. More precisely, in that office my friends jokingly called Heaven, either because it commanded Paris from on high, or for moral reasons.

I was at that time a manuscript reader at ***, working in one of its children's imprints. My office was flooded with file folders full of unpublished manuscripts. There were no, or almost no, published books at my place, no finished books. Those that surrounded me still had need of me: I loved them for that, I suppose. (*A contrario*, let us posit a *normal* library—we say, quite rightly, with the same sense of describing the bizarre: a *normal* childhood—containing Dumas *père*, Jules Verne, etc., with the proviso that this library is merely *potential*.) For I relished this climate of uncertainty, sustained—for however long I could continue saying no and yet not leave off toying with and rummaging through these texts that appealed at worst to my naivete, and at best to my affections—by what might be called problems or stumbling blocks.

In all honesty, it wasn't so much the power (which might be deemed excessive, but which was, for lack of a better excuse, by no means unusual) that mattered to me as problems such as the following: This young Araucanian boy who traveled down the Neuquén River in search of a legendary lost city, would he *or wouldn't he* fire the imaginations of other children—speaking here on behalf of what, if not a childhood I had to find inside myself, for lack of being the proper age?—with wonder and delight?

One could, therefore, have accused me of a taste for the incomplete. I'm referring here to those flawed texts guilty of various sins. These could still be chastised. Hence they still offered room for my correction, over and above, in short, their present state of disgrace. I felt at home within this space. Accordingly, I saw to it that the aperture was always closed as late in the procedure as possible. I would leave the disjointed manuscript lying open on the table, utterly dependent on me, until the very last moment—the way Angelica is always rescued—for its beauty and survival. As an unfortunate result, I was thought spineless.

Here one might say I'm deliberately pitting the reader against me. But I'm merely bowing to necessity, inasmuch as these few weaknesses explain the adventure to follow. I trust I'll be forgiven for ending this catalog on a detail that, though hardly the most descriptive, seems to me to lend weight to the rest (perhaps for what it implies about correction and, again, about taste): As all the file folders that came my way were of different, vivid, and—at least to me—arbitrary colors, I'd undertaken to provide them, in my office on rue de H., a blank white background.

This same concern for bringing the reader in with open eyes and in full possession of the facts obliges me to confess yet another gentle madness: I collected seashells. (This detail is included to justify certain oddities in the relationships I was to form with several key players in the case.) I say *gentle* because experience has taught me that this particular weakness—a means of compensating for the barely concealed animosity elicited by my role as censor—often earned me a measure of sympathy (most likely because people were pleased to discover that I had a chink in my armor, that a certain amount of compassion for me was possible, given the state of perpetual dissatisfaction to which I had consigned myself, that even so I was a man of hope, etc.). Consequently, people set in opposition two endeavors that were actually quite similar, in my view, both being marked by an obsession with what can only be called perfection, or the absolute, as my life's work stemmed from the dual infinities of seashells lacking from my collection and errors not to be countenanced.

One day a female friend, S., spotted at a glance something out of the ordinary in this room devoted to study. It was the presence of multiple empty packets of Gauloises cigarettes (eleven in all, if I'm not mistaken, strewn about haphazardly through my own negligence). Needless to say, I hadn't noticed them. But now they struck me with as much force as they had S.: isolated spots of pale blue, quite obvious—so blindingly obvious, in fact, that they caused me a vague perturbation, more or less akin to that which might be induced by a carefully arranged *vanitas* still life. That was the day, I think, when the idea of seashells first came to me. I suppose I was hoping to preserve the unsettling but ultimately pleasurable effect, while at the same time ridding it of the lingering suggestion of slovenliness that was hardly to my credit. At any rate, I began by placing a few abalone shells (souvenirs cast up onto a forgettable beach visited on vacation, and as such doubly dross, yet fine specimens, and surpassingly delicate . . .) in the selfsame places to which I'd unconsciously relegated my old cigarette packets. (And these were, in fact, examples of those curious places that exist in every room and that God-knows-what personal aversion condemns to perpetual abandonment: somehow no hand ever visits them.) Then I sought out other, analogous places through long trial and error, and other shells.

Of course, the choice was not entirely innocent. And this is surely not the place to rehearse all the various connotations such objects might carry for a *man of literature*. Suffice it to say that, as time wore on, I was to draw from this collection a satisfaction far less abstract than that of seeing in it the toothing stones, for example, of never-ending architectures. No, this satisfaction touched on matters of the heart: When newcomers entered my office on rue de H., I don't know whether or not they experienced the vertiginous effect described above. But, then again, I rarely had to wait long before I'd see evidence of a strange temptation coming over them. A temptation perhaps linked to the fact that my objects, far from being neatly ranged on a couple of shelves, and thereby designated off-limits, were distributed seemingly at random, in all sorts of unlikely places, washed ashore by some impossible tide. In any case, at some point in our conversation it was almost inevitable that my visitor would feel the urge to pick up a shell. (Which at times they would do casually—as if something about the gesture were a foregone conclusion, a necessity so overwhelming that no explanation was needed—and at other times in a more self-conscious or playful manner, according to the degree of rapport between us, and the act dared, in the best of cases, to answer the desire in full, i.e., putting the shell up to an ear, where it would supposedly re-echo the sound of the sea.) I came to look forward to this childlike gesture of which I had, privately, made a ritual, perhaps even a litmus test, and enjoy it more than anything on earth—and some people were perceptive enough to suspect that I saw it as a sign of allegiance. But why not instead call it camaraderie, or love?

More than by way of warning or disclaimer, I mention all this because, today, my most vivid memory of that office my friends used to call *Heaven* is perhaps this strange procession of young men and women with my seashells pressed to their ears—and I so joyous opposite.

Nevertheless, the point of departure for this whole affair wasn't a visit at all. Perhaps one might even say it was the *reverse*. In early May of 19--, an unremarkable manuscript arrived in the mail for me, to which I initially paid no particular attention. (To tell the truth, I'd received several manuscripts that day and was regarding them with a certain degree of ill humor, owing to the fact that I was just then preparing to use up the balance of my vacation days and had promised myself I'd go to O. unencumbered by either work or guilt.) Doubtless I would have left it unopened on my desk along with the rest, if a random (and frankly silly) mishap hadn't intervened. To wit:

It was often my custom during the course of the day to drink a glass of scalded milk, the only thing capable of overcoming a tendency to daydream which was hardly compatible with the demands of exercising critical judgment. Now, on this particular afternoon— owing to stress, absent-mindedness brought on by my impending departure for O., or what have you—my glass was apparently overfilled: I left a ridiculous milk ring on the packet where I had set it down.

Obviously, this incident was of absolutely no importance in and of itself. But it irked me. Besides, ever since the business with the Gauloises, I'd been maintaining a certain discipline (I didn't do a great deal of tidying as such, but laziness, as it happened, along with the necessity I was under not to allow anyone in my office who might disturb my things, had led me to a compromise: I would smoke less, write on the backs of my rough drafts in a very small hand, refrain from crumpling my waste paper into balls: in short, I would preserve a semblance of neatness and order). And so, infuriated by the task I was going to leave behind (I mentally appended: *for such a long time*), I tried blotting, wiping, rubbing, etc., with the end result that I tore off the ruined envelope entirely, because it was the simplest solution. It was in this blockheaded way that I made the acquaintance of Desiderio.

In truth, *made the acquaintance of* is the wrong term. Not only because the author of the manuscript I found beneath the torn paper revealed nothing whatsoever about himself, but also because the ostentatious name he'd chosen as his pseudonym was already well-known to me, indeed quite well-known for quite some time.

It had already been several years since I'd stumbled across a remarkable canvas by chance on a visit to the Museum of Decorative Arts, by a painter of whom I then knew nothing. The canvas was Monsù Desiderio's magnificent *Ruined Landscape*. It's well known: eerie parvises in the gloaming, in wait for some ineffable mystery, the left facade barred (why?) by a large shadow in the shape of a Saint Andrew's cross. So moved had I been by this painting that I'd scoured several art-history books for information on its creator. I even compiled a bibliography of secondary sources.* All of which, far from providing me with answers, only raised further questions. For example: What to make of that bizarre *bottega*, the Barra–De Nome duo, one painting tranquil cities and the other their apocalypses, God and Devil joined under a single name in seventeenth-century Naples? This *Monsieur Didier* was a labyrinth.

Nonetheless, compilation work of this kind was unlike me. And I'd never seriously wanted to produce an in-depth study on my painter: that would have been beyond my abilities. On the other hand, I did feel dogged by the idea of writing some sort of fictional work on the subject of, or in the style of, Desiderio—something like what poets and musicians call a *tombeau*. I don't know why I found this artwork so magical, such a fraternal spirit. I suppose that, faced with those fractured or incomplete landscapes, it was gratifying to be able to apply my own cement . . . In hindsight, I think this reaction was in perfect keeping with my character. In any case, only the lack of time and the multiplicity of other professional interests prevented me from writing this book, one of those which, as they say, we all *have in us* like children waiting to be born.

Imagine my surprise, then, on receiving a manuscript in the name of the unknown master who had become my obsession. My surprise, and my sudden interest.

....

* Including J. Height's study of *Explosion in a Cathedral*, the Allomello collection catalog, the works of Profs. Romdahl and Causa, those of Sluys published by Minotaure, three articles by Dr. W. in the *Revue Médicale*, selected extracts of Marcel Brion's *Art Fantastique*, etc.

Monsù Desiderio—I didn't yet know him by any other name—had done everything in his power to pique my curiosity. I should say, rather: to rope me into this mad story, because a number of other, equally disquieting coincidences gave me reason to suspect a deliberate plan at work under the cover of literature. I even thought someone might be trying to take me for a ride, so to speak, but I had no acquaintance intimate enough to divine my secret urges and repressed emotions, which I'd confided to no one. An example: The brief, typewritten cover letter that accompanied the manuscript gave one Alban Lievel as a reference. Now, if I didn't know Lievel personally, his name was at least familiar to me and, more importantly, gave rise to very mixed feelings—unmentioned, if not unmentionable—that deserve further elaboration.

I hold Lievel's books in the highest esteem, but at the time this tale begins, I was most keenly aware of him as my predecessor at ***, a fellow manuscript reader who'd left under very mysterious circumstances. As far as I was able to piece together from conversations with mutual friends, office gossip, and the pseudo-autobiographical short stories written by Lievel himself, the motives behind his departure had to do with certain qualms and, first and foremost, with the growth of an uncontrollable bent.

In the weeks leading up to the break, Lievel had adopted, or pretended to adopt, an attitude of unqualified admiration for increasingly shallow, increasingly vile art ("idiotic paintings . . . badly spelled pornography, the novels of our grandmothers . . ."—we all know the temptation) and it didn't seem to be from mere dandyism or a taste for provocation. I'd also definitively ruled out the idea, overly simplistic in my view, that it was some sort of weakening of the critical faculties, the way one's eyesight deteriorates with age, prolonged exposure to bright sunlight, or darkness. I was determined to find another explanation, and from this it would be fair to deduce that I was projecting (with all the more ease for my object being a stranger, someone with whom I'd never raised a glass, who'd never taken the opportunity, during a philosophical discussion, to flourish a dirty magazine under my nose in order to *see my eyes*—*sic*, from the portrait of Lievel sketched by one acquaintance) of one of my own proclivities onto him. I'm referring primarily to my weakness for *flawed* books. They unquestionably allowed me—more so than *finished* books, which couldn't help but leave me feeling dispirited, empty, and superfluous—to take the measure of—and live up to—my full potential (I'm speaking here in the broader sense, with no particular regard to my profession, nothing being more abhorrent to me than a book which affords no glimpse of a better one: I would flounder, sink, and drown in such a book).

Hence the idea, and I took Lievel as a case in point, that such a predilection, which I still had more than enough mettle to resist, could potentially metastasize into an out-and-out mania. All it took was to let oneself become a little too enamored of some minor imperfection, a little too ready to see it as a blessing in disguise, to say that, by comparison, the finished work of art was a theft, a stripping bare, etc. First symptom: Lievel's stubborn insistence on giving an exhaustive account of his condition (the way people will try to quell a persistent itch or stomach pain by parading it before others in an unseemly manner, somewhere between a fond reminiscence and a wisecrack). Then Lievel had departed, because, in the end, this complaint is a fatal one.

That, in a nutshell, was what Lievel's case boiled down to, in my opinion. You can see why I was torn. He'd gotten carried away in the same way I had, I suppose. This is probably what lies behind the animus one feels toward the former lover of the woman one loves, who as such was the first to discover the secret kink or signature sexual move one would have liked, above all other exclusivities, to reserve eternally for oneself. I hadn't gone to see him when I'd started at ***. But for the same reason I'd avoided him then, I'd often wanted to meet him since. (To discuss *it*, of course. To discuss it . . . or to convince myself I wasn't heading for the same disappointments? Or, alternatively, to differentiate my struggles from his? Or perhaps to make sure the signs I'd noticed didn't indicate a dispossession?)

That Desiderio—who'd given me the pretext I needed to see Lievel—would play the role of intermediary regarding an urge I'd kept so close, and especially after having hit on such a significant name, did not fail to astonish me. But what made me laugh was that such phenomenal coincidences would have all come to naught, and I would have gone off to O., leaving the problem of liking or disliking his book to others, if I hadn't demonstrated, on that particular day, such doltish clumsiness.

I read through the manuscript that very night. As the reference to Lievel had made me suspect, it wasn't really in my line. What I mean is, it obviously wasn't a children's book. (I smiled at the idea of N., who managed the imprint and whose prescriptions I had in mind—a dash of history, a pinch of geographical information on the Loyalty Islands or somewhere even more remote, almost nothing of the fantastic or supernatural: in a word, what's known as educational literature, with our young Araucanian being a prime example—reading these pages.) In fact, it wasn't even technically a book. Desiderio's manuscript was untitled. It was also extremely short: about twenty typed pages, and I thought to myself how difficult it would be, coming from an unknown author, to justify the publication of this slender pamphlet, even under one of our other imprints. Nonetheless, it didn't lack for interest. Except for the anomaly of the chosen pseudonym, which might appear to some wholly unmerited, and the fact that if I had been expecting the evocation of a setting between life and death, with strange suns and tumbling vaults whose impacts one awaited in vain (it was only natural that I would presumptively ascribe to a text as problematic as this one my own literary orientations), I was sorely disappointed.

On the other hand, I was able to put my mind at ease on one score, at least. Though I'd begun by leafing through my nameless guest rather timidly, in passing, whenever my habitual movements chanced to take me past the table where the manuscript lay—getting up to make a glass of milk, opening the window to clear the smoke of yet another cigarette—because I had a vague dread of finding written there the very things *I needed* to say, in fact it contained nothing of the kind. The text dealt with a completely different subject (and so, in my naivete [or flippancy?], I vowed to let this pseudo-Desiderio know that his choice of name was sheer pretentiousness.)

In relaxed, informal language, occasionally incorrect but artful nonetheless, the text presented the portrait of a woman. The author endowed her with a name as melodramatic as it was affected: *Belladonna*, or in some instances: *La Belle Dame*, at which I couldn't help but smile. And I was struck by two things. First, at no point was there any physical description of the lady, a fact which became apparent only on close examination, the reader having initially sensed nothing more than an ill-defined absence. Her character was depicted through a few revealing gestures, emotions, and situations that defied all logical interpretation (and here I was strangely reminded of the moment in certain detective novels when the victim's body is found and is suddenly understood to be lifeless because the hand, or neck, is positioned at an *impossible angle*). Hence the ambiguous (shameful?) sensation one might feel at the idea of a beautiful female corpse (though no death actually occurred).

The second thing that troubled me had to do with the memories such extraordinary situations stirred up in me. Not that I'd ever lived them, far from it—were they even capable of being lived?—but I'd lived others, substantially similar, the elements of which it seemed to me I found scattered throughout in a new order. And it's true that this reading, when all was said and done, left me in a *disordered* state—if I might so interpret, for example, my unprompted rearranging of several nearby seashells, something I never do as a rule, and other minor lapses of that evening, none of any great moment.

To give a better idea of what these passages were like and how they resonated with me, I can readily summon a personal memory (all the more appropriate for the fact that my first reaction was the thought that this memory would not *detract from* Desiderio's text). It's true that this isn't, strictly speaking, a *true* memory, but rather a dream, and as such both *a priori* indefensible and perfectly in keeping with my correspondent's style. I can only hope that this reason alone will suffice to pardon the account that follows, should the reader detest as much as I do the recounting of dreams in books, as being cheaply poetic, arbitrary, insubstantial, and irrelevant.

Several months before receiving Desiderio's letter-bomb, I'd broken off all relations with C. Since that time, there had been no other woman in my life. I wouldn't say I was suffering, per se, but my fingers were aching with nonexistent caresses, and I suppose my contact with things was altered in consequence. I mention this because I believe this sort of situation predisposes one to having certain recurring dreams, and to having them more frequently. That was how, during this interim period, I ended up dreaming the following three or four times:

I'm in a smallish room which appears to be a library. It's nothing like my *Heaven* because the walls aren't bare but lined with something. Books, I believe: valuable, leather-bound books. But I don't go closer to verify. Really, it's just an impression—if there is such a thing as the impression of being surrounded by leather-bound books. The room is hot. It's hot and, though I'm certainly no expert in psychology, I feel confident in characterizing the space as *womblike*. I'm seated in an extremely soft armchair, but I can't be sure of this detail, either: no one turns around, in dreams, to see what's supporting them. The table at which I'm seated holds an assortment of objects. There's a closed door on my left and a French door directly in front of me, which I know leads to a small garden in a more or less total state of neglect, choked with weeds and full of old junk, even though none of this is visible to me at the moment. The French door is ajar.

Presently a woman enters through the door on the left. (I make a move to protect the loose sheets of paper around me from a possible draft, but I needn't have bothered.) I judge this woman to be quite beautiful, but I couldn't give any more specific description of her than that: whatever I said, I would be unfaithful. As often happens in dreams, her image is reduced to the emotion it engenders. For, though I have a conviction of beauty in her presence, everything else about her escapes me. Better—or worse—yet, I'm positive I don't desire this very beautiful woman.

The woman isn't particularly surprised to see me here. Nor am I to see her, for beyond a doubt, and without my being able to say whether the expectation stems from signs within the dream itself or from its unvarying repetition, I'd been expecting her. She walks over to me. She looks at me with undisguised weariness. We remain like this for several seconds without speaking. Then, reaching across the table cluttered with objects, I hand her a leather bag, a woman's handbag, which I can only assume is hers. She takes it and thanks me. Upon which, before I can make the slightest move or begin to formulate the explanation that in any case eludes me, my visitor disappears out the back, through the French door. That's the last I see of her.

Nearly everyone is familiar with those dreams in which, being intent on prompt action, you find yourself bogged down, held fast, or otherwise impeded by an uncooperative environment redolent of death. In a like manner, at this point I attempt to stand, if only to warn the fleeing woman—for lack of any other message—that this is the wrong way out, that she risks cutting her legs to ribbons on the brambles or tripping over family heirlooms full of nails and broken glass, as I'm afraid she might. But I'm hampered by all sorts of obstacles, of which the worst is the table between me and the French door. And so my increasingly frantic efforts to liberate myself pull me irresistibly—I know this already for having suffered the same misadventure two or three times before—toward consciousness. I wake in a cold sweat. And that's it.

That's it as far as the dream is concerned. But the dream is not, perhaps, the strangest part of the affair, nor even that which best justifies the comparison I've made, but rather this detail: on waking, I'd invariably notice that an ejaculation had occurred during my sleep—to all appearances near its end. I knew this was fairly normal after a long period of abstinence (among monks, for example, or soldiers garrisoned in some remote rural town)—my split with C. was by then long past. What remained a mystery to me had to do with the total absence of erotic stimuli in the images the dream so stubbornly insisted on showing me. Because, I repeat, the woman with the bag, despite being perfectly beautiful, was *undesirable* to me. As for the final anxiety, could anyone seriously argue that it had sexual overtones? And I asked myself this question, which might seem stupid: Had I felt any pleasure?

For it was just this sort of deeply troubling incongruity that haunted Desiderio's text.

This brief overview of the coincidences that emerged between the manuscript torn by chance from its dirty wrapper and my own personal preoccupations will suffice—I hope—to explain my discomfiture.

Subsequently, of course, I tried to find a rational explanation. Such as: I might have been dropping references to Desiderio left and right, speaking aloud, on the street, for example, with a bravado that may seem ludicrous, in front of a bizarrely cracked building slated for demolition, the fine old name of De Nome—in which case someone had taken me at my word. To believe that the reference to Lievel was deliberately aimed at my most sensitive nerve amounted to a denial that Lievel, simply because he was willing to throw his life away, could also have friends. As for the dream, it was, on the whole, nothing more than an illustrative example. It was I who had drawn a parallel between it and the manuscript, and on the basis of very tenuous analogies at that (maybe what they came down to, ultimately, was the anonymity of the female character, a character I was certain, in both cases, that I knew—but not her features, nor her voice, nor her habits: knew *what*, then?). I was forgetting that such resonances can simply be the sign of a good book.

(To stay on the subject of this dream, I briefly flirted with another theory: Knowing little about psychoanalysis but convinced that there were several clear obsessions in evidence to which analysis might give me the key, I sent a complete account to an old friend who'd studied under Professor W. In truth, even though we'd been, in elementary and then secondary school in J., like true brothers, I'd long since lost touch with this friend. I wasn't surprised to receive no reply. Afterward, however, I was kicking myself for having made a confession of such magnitude so casually. Anyone would have laughed to see how I squirmed at the idea of my story being trotted out as an anecdote or a case study in somebody's living room, the devil knows where, before an audience of strangers. I know it's ridiculous, but I really did start to wonder: Could Desiderio have been among them?)

Faced, as I believe, with a captivating creative vision, a fantasia, my imagination was reduced to inventing the plausible. I was so conscious of this inversion that I almost let the many anomalies with no direct bearing on my secret tastes fall forgotten by the wayside. Such as: Why did Desiderio submit to an editor of children's books a text that, however one looked at it, was addressed to an adult sensibility? Why did he confine himself to such a brief sample, one that admitted no possibility of publication? Why did he dash it off in such haste (in my opinion, the manuscript hadn't had the benefit of any preliminary drafts or revisions, hence its errors) when he demonstrated evident skill—what I've called *artfulness*— at his craft? And a corollary question: Was this an author who'd already *made a name for himself* and felt he had to conceal it? To further what sort of hoax, which no one would find funny?

I set the manuscript aside and left it untouched all the next day. I read a few very different works and made use of a theater ticket someone had given me, because experience had taught me that a text will carry a different meaning after you've let yourself be carried away by others. I was probably hoping the former would seem more laughable (but then this sacred music, this beloved book, were perhaps nothing more than the means of escaping a growing sympathy for the lively, expressive manuscript by making it seem puerile). I reread it.

The result was that I became all the more convinced, not only of the affinities linking me to Desiderio, but also of a compelling urgency behind his unexpected missive. I would say I'd persuaded myself that it was, for lack of a better word, a kind of appeal. I was thinking of some deep loneliness, or a friend's emotional blackmail, or those burning confessions for which a close acquaintance or priest would have been, for reasons I couldn't begin to fathom, deemed unworthy. I still didn't believe there was any danger.

But no matter how resolved I was, on finishing this rereading, to contact Lievel and pursue my investigation as far as I could, I remember resisting the idea, in spite of it all (in the following way: I took the opportunity to underline the manuscript's errors with red felt-tip pen, to cover it with *dele* marks—heedless of the injury such a show of authority might do to a young man's pride—as if it were a child's school assignment). I resisted after my own fashion.

II

I put off my trip to O. for at least another week. This was possible, even easy, because it was yet only May, a cold and rainy May in Paris. In O., booking a room in advance wasn't strictly necessary. (I liked to take my vacations in May for the freedom it afforded. I'd think to myself, *I'm leaving for O. on Sunday*, but the thought wouldn't carry the force of conviction. By *O.*, I would also mean all the other towns I was at liberty to choose in its stead between then and Sunday. They were superposed inside me, hotel upon hotel, house upon house, as in the most precarious utopias. There I wended my way through many delicate itineraries. Until Sunday, that is, when I'd have to resolve the dilemma of these manifold imagined Troys, all so beautiful, but so tightly intertwined that to excavate one would be to eviscerate another—loss was unavoidable.) In the meantime, I carried out a full-fledged investigation.

I arranged to meet with friends. As many as possible. Over meals, in cafés, at my place, at their offices. It had been a year since I'd seen some of them. This long, extraordinary cortege of friends spanned the entire week of my postponement. They received me warmly. They were pleasantly surprised to see me, having thought I was away on vacation. They'd be wearing suits, I a sweater jacket. We'd sit down at a table and, because the weather was overcast even at midday, there would always be a lit lamp beside us.

Our conversations weren't altogether natural, as I was concealing the real reasons behind them. Though we gave needless little synopses of the months we'd been apart, the time was not yet ripe for emotional outpourings. Sentences begun would not necessarily be finished, because the undertaking was still in progress, so that I started to wonder: Is it possible for so few undertakings to be completed within a year? Then my friend, losing his voice, would pick up some nearby object—a lighter, an ashtray, or, if at my place, a seashell—and gently toy with it.

My thinking was that one of them must have played a leading role in the Desiderio affair. That is, if he wasn't Desiderio himself (on this count, I reproached myself for having lost or burned all their letters, which might have revealed handwriting idiosyncrasies or incorrigible telltale errors). Since a rather vain sensitivity forbade me from putting the question to them point-blank, I used these comfortable silences to lay snares for them. For example: I knew the manuscript had been mailed from V. on 30 April, the postmark attesting as much. V. being a good distance from Paris, I might say to my friend that it seemed to me I'd seen him at the Porte Dorée train station on the 30th (or at the Brasserie Lipp, or La Cartoucherie—and this was exactly how I imagined Lievel subjecting him to a photograph of genitals or breasts: to see his eyes). But he was never thrown off balance: the sighting was either possible or it wasn't, but in neither case would he let slip any detail betraying a potential voyage to V., on the coast. Or this: I'd tell him I'd found my dream house and invent a description on the fly. When he asked me where it was, I'd say: "11 rue de Nazareth, in V.": true or false, this was the address given by Desiderio, which I'd found on a piece of the torn wrapper. My friend would congratulate me.

I'd talk about Lievel. I'd pretend—in order to furnish grist for a discussion that was remarkably lacking in material ever since Lievel had retired and stopped writing—to share, sometimes, his atrocious taste. My friend wouldn't answer right away. Then, when pressed:

"I thought," he'd say, "Lievel was dead."

It was quite a week. I spent it imagining the specters of my friends haunting every subway station in Paris, at times when they were, perhaps, peacefully at home making love. Nonetheless, I continued to erect villas of pure fantasy for their benefit on rue de Nazareth in V.—word of my newfound wealth must have already been spreading. At any rate, these same friends would lose their tongues, ten times out of ten, the moment the conversation turned to Lievel, if they didn't instead reach for a glass or a seashell and hold it in silence, the same way, in truth, one might clasp the hand of a bereaved friend (which was all the more ridiculous because Lievel, as I would soon prove, was alive and well. What was it, then?).

Perhaps they were merely trying to convey that the *author* was dead. Too, they might have felt a discomfort regarding him akin to my own. But the sadness, I thought, came primarily from me. On subjects relating to Desiderio—my lie of omission—everything I'd told my friends was pure fiction. As a result, I said my farewells, time and again, with the same basic feeling: I'd injured them. Nevertheless, I would go out that very evening to meet another friend, with the customary suit and the lamp at his elbow, and my sole concern would be to deliver the same untruths in a slightly more plausible form. All the while asking myself: Why?

The time not taken up with friends was dedicated to the hunt for Lievel. Here I ran into difficulties. Whenever I presented myself at an address someone had given me, the door would be answered by a very young man who would say: "What do you want?"

He would invariably be a small-town boy. He'd just moved to Paris a month ago: he was obviously still living in a dream. He didn't know the former occupant, though he did have a souvenir or two—a comb forgotten in the back of a cabinet, for example, or an old pair of shoes wrapped in yellowed newspaper (and—he didn't say this aloud, but I could infer it: dirty laundry, nail clippings, etc., the seamy side of the Lievel I was after, from certain contemptuous glances he would give me). Then he'd shut the door in my face as if I were a traveling salesman, this very young man having no need of anything.

All these young men reminded me so strongly of the inhabitants of rue Houdon (from back when I was searching for traces of C. de M. and those two invaluable detached houses described by Thierry: "The one on the right is occupied by a charming billiard room hung with architecture painted on canvas. The ceiling depicts a heavenly sky ..."): surly and skeptical to a degree fully commensurate with my own disappointment, which was considerable enough—nothing at all remained of those beautiful houses—that I now felt I was investigating an equally barren past, as if Lievel no longer existed save in a prospective memory, because I was willing it so. Even at the risk of wasting his time.

Owing either to this, or to my fraudulently friendly visits, or to the absurd uncertainty of my situation (was I or wasn't I on vacation?), I was preoccupied all week, tormented by swarms of unaccustomed qualms, desires, and anxieties (which had always seemed to me like those of a child *raising a fuss* when faced with an escalator or a crosswalk—they were examples of those extraordinary emotions that have a startling quality peculiar to childhood, and they rattled me). To such an extent that my absent-mindedness was playing untold tricks on me like the following:

I was in a subway tunnel between two spurious addresses of Lievel's, lost in my reflections, when I barged into a stranger (who was probably looking the other way in an attempt to get his bearings). And on doing so, instead of saying "Pardon me," I muttered something like "shellfish," or maybe "Desiderio." It took me a good ten seconds to register the incoherence of what I'd said and to feel that I should try and persuade the man that I was sane. But by this time he was so far away, and I was so uncertain of being able to pick him out from among the other commuters that I stood there petrified by this thought: How, other than by a chase that would itself seem deranged, and then a flood of fervent protests that would initially defy belief, could I ever have convinced the man I wasn't a lunatic?

This mishap gives some idea of my day-to-day activities during that week spent in the margins, a week full of bolts from the blue—much like, when half-asleep, one follows one's own unanswerable logic, and later wonders: Did I completely lose my judgment, or was I, in fact, more rational than reason itself?—at the end of which—week or logic—almost by accident, I was to discover the retreat I'd been seeking.

One building caretaker I questioned had, miraculously, preserved a possible address for Lievel in an almanac from the previous year. It was in Montmartre. I went there the following Saturday, still persuaded that Lievel—who had clearly not taken the trouble to have his (hypothetical) mail forwarded—had given out false information. (In the meantime, I'd learned from the *** Press's accounting department that all correspondence addressed to Lievel for the past five years, concerning—most notably—a standing credit balance of FF---, had come back marked "unknown at this address," and so I was pursuing this lead solely from a sense of duty, or, as they say, for the glory.) This is all to explain the following: that I was not altogether prepared for this encounter, which was to be such an important one: I was instead expecting the door to be opened by yet another young man. But Lievel really was living on the impasse E. des B. And I trust I'll be excused, at this point in the Desiderio case, for setting down so minutely and so clumsily—according to the emotionality I associated above with childhood—the circumstances of this lone interview, in the questionable order furnished by my memory.

First of all, if it's true that I was expecting another young man—small town, shoes, happiness, etc.—I must have thought that this door on the top floor of the alley side of the building, like the doors of apartment blocks undergoing demolition that open onto the void, opened onto time. What I mean is, going straight from the happy young man to the unworthy old man that was Lievel was enough to make one's heart sink.

Since I'd seen him only in old press clippings, I was also confronted by the vision of a familiar face suddenly withered and wasted. We all know the turn our reflection in a shop window can give us if glimpsed unexpectedly, that is to say, minus the usual mental safeguards with which we typically gird ourselves when approaching a mirror: shocking.

And perhaps over time I'd adopted this simple line of reasoning from my friends: How could a man with such an appetite for words survive his own silence? With the result that I was thinking: Here's where someone will finally give me confirmation of his death.

Instead of which, Lievel stood before me in the flesh, looking almost comical (if that was compatible with the surreal feeling mentioned above: I recall that, as soon as I'd recovered from my embarrassment, the first thing I noticed was that the buttons of his woolen vest had been done up wrong: they were all off by one buttonhole. I'd pictured him as a tall man, but he was appreciably shorter than I was. His glasses' frames were hopelessly out of date. I was the one dripping with rain, but it was he who seemed to be coming in from outdoors, etc.).

Disconcerted, I extended him my hand without a word, as if the success of my efforts must have been just as dazzling to him as it was to me. He shook it uncomprehendingly. And it was only after this absurd handshake that I stated, by way of justification, the fact of the FF--- that had been owing him for so long. And, reversing our reputations as if it were *he* who ought to know *me*, my name.

The old man led me down a hall into the apartment. He offered me a seat in the middle of a large, glassed-in room, which looked to me like it had once been an artist's studio of the kind they used to make from the converted lofts of venerable old Parisian buildings. The disorder that reigned here irritated me. I don't know whether there were multiple empty cigarette packets lying around, but I do remember having the nagging thought that it wouldn't take more than a slight relaxation of my vigilance for my nice, neat office on rue de H. to become like this pigsty. (One day when I was working by the fireplace and one of my papers fell into the flames, I wrestled for a long moment with a strange temptation to toss in after it the entire manuscript, which represented a full year's work, thinking to myself, with a kind of morbid curiosity: Could I destroy, just like that, the thing around which my life has been organized for so long? A little foretaste of suicide: the large room of the impasse E. des B.)

I didn't bring up Desiderio right away. There was no need: Lievel seemed eager to talk about our mutual acquaintances, both at *** and elsewhere. I gamely supplied several diplomatic anecdotes, though I had to bellow them on account of the rain beating against the glass (our entire conversation was amplified in this way). I noticed there was no lamp on the table.

I did, however, notice several trashy magazines, a few pop novels, some ugly wood furniture with water rings, a couple of overdoor paintings, the remains of a half-eaten breakfast, and the blue-tinted windowpanes—we were blue as well—like light bulbs during the war.

It was Lievel who, little by little, brought the conversation around to books. What he said confirmed my suppositions so completely that, for a moment, it sounded implausible, or like an elaborate setup. (I mean to say: Suppose I invent a fatal accident as part of a story. Then I walk out my front door and witness an identical accident. My first thought will obviously be that a movie is being shot on rue de H., and I'll expect one of the bit players to tell me to move along. One of Lievel's paradoxical pronouncements—such as "my poetry robs others of the fundamental right to speak it aloud" and whatnot—was this fatal accident. Someone, if logic was any guide, would soon be telling me to act natural for the cameras, to pretend I believed in these words as in the glass debris, the red, the broken body of a woman.) I behaved exactly as they would have wanted, which is to say, not disrupting the continuity of the events that would foreseeably ensue in response, but also not participating in them any more than would an ordinary passerby.

I noted to myself that Lievel was using the same arguments I myself had used on my friends only the day before (though in my case it had been solely to keep them talking long enough to betray themselves). Now that I was answering in their place, giving the same replies they had given me, I began to wonder: What part in what deception was I, in turn, attempting to cover up?

This conversation, or rather this monologue of Lievel's—I did nothing but supply the *requisite* responses—went on for about an hour. Night was falling fast. The rain continued to pour down: we were positively shouting. It was inevitable that sooner or later Lievel would put me on trial. Sauce for the reader is sauce for the writer. I knew this. I was so well prepared for it that to me it was child's play: I could have fed him his lines. Then I would have said that we all act as policeman to someone, and even worse . . .

And yet I let him go on, without at first really knowing why. It wasn't weariness. It wasn't even because I'd lost interest in the discussion, or out of respect. In hindsight, I think the darkness was helping me rediscover a long-lost and delicious sense of certainty:

Once, in another big old house (from my childhood: it was big because I was small), an equally caustic scolding had left me no room for doubt—as strident as the accusing voice had been, so must the censured pleasure have been proportionately unprecedented— that I was *guilty at last*. The reason I didn't answer Lievel was for this pleasure and this certainty. All I did, when I felt his sarcasm rising, was, like my friends, pick up a small object within easy reach (some kitschy *objet d'art* or tabloid rag), not in a casual way, but as if it were a sign that should have been as familiar to my interlocutor as his reprimands were to me, and turn it gently in my hands.

Given that the invective simply rolled off my back and the voice making itself heard over the rain was providing the aforementioned pleasure, I wound up listening to the sound of this voice alone. Since Lievel could no longer see my eyes, I took the opportunity to examine the room around me. And, in doing so, instead of trying to appreciate it, I indulged (however rude and, in particular, however narrow-minded such an attitude may seem) in mentally remodeling it to suit my own taste (for example: I replaced the panes tinted for passive defense with clear glass. I refaced the walls in roughcast plaster. I used the buffet table for firewood and replaced it with a low sideboard holding a basket of oranges) as I waited for the voice to reach a crescendo, either in self-vindication (?) or because of the downpour (?) or as a way of calling me to order (?)—which would have excited more than embarrassed me, since it would have called up some stirring memories.

As I was still smiling to myself over this idea, Lievel snapped on a small table lamp sitting atop a stack of crime novels. Without realizing it, I'd been fondling an obscene statuette of the kind found in shops that sell junky Indian bric-a-brac. I suppose it was to regain my composure, albeit somewhat stupidly—or to explain my smile, but explain it how?—that I asked Lievel straight out whether he knew Desiderio.

This bluntness, the result of having been so brutally wrenched from my childhood home, paid off more handsomely than all my prior beating around the bush: If I'd ever thought Lievel might have had a hand in what I regarded as a bad joke, his present astonishment would have persuaded me otherwise. I told him about the manuscript, the various coincidences. He said: "No. There's no one who could list me as a reference. Between you and me: Who would find it in his interest to do so?"

"A friend. Someone who must have visited you and thought seeing your name would suffice for me."

"You said he wasn't *the type*."

"I could be wrong."

"No address?"

"Rue de Nazareth, in V."

He asked whether I had the manuscript on me. I was about to give it to him when an inexplicable reservation stopped me: at the risk of seeming discourteous, I settled for reading him a few passages aloud. He listened attentively. I watched his face as I read, this time without any corrections, the aforementioned errors (still in a very loud voice, to the point that, in my weakness, I felt the need to exculpate myself afterward). His eyes were closed, and I remember that this attitude of calm, so absurd in the midst of all that noise, made me stumble over my words several times. When I'd finished, he remained silent for a long time (and I felt an urge to pick up the statuette again, as if by doing so I could have proven … what, exactly?) before saying: "I used to know someone in V. He was originally from there, I believe. Morelle. Jean Morelle. And it's true, he did write."

"Do you think he could be the author of this?"

"Anyone can be the author of anything."

(In truth, he added with the barest hint of a smile that he, Lievel, could have been the author of *Paradise Lost* or *The Theory of the Four Movements*, that he'd missed his luck …)

"Yes, but do you think …"

"It's probably his."

"And the name Desiderio?"

"There's a remarkable museum in V. dedicated to utopias, and it has the *Circular Landscape* from the Tassinari-Chatel bequest. The name was there for the taking."

Since my host's answers grew singularly terse after this exchange, I didn't venture to question him any further. But I knew from experience that a long silence could elicit unexpected confidences, the very kind, I thought, I needed at this moment. So I let the silence build, suppressing all signs of discomfort, staring innocently at a corner of the room (which couldn't help but be a site of disorder or discord: I remember water pissing through the cracked glass roof into a faux-Gien vase) until the figure of Desiderio-Morelle—what Lievel knew of him—should be born out of the intolerable strain: in which I was not mistaken.

And so I learned that this individual was not a person dear to Lievel's heart (but for the extremely specious reasons already known, and therefore what could I make of such a judgment, which was so at odds with a text that attested, in the end, to such vulnerability?). He'd known him in Paris, when the young writer, trying to find an identity, had come to ask his advice. Lievel had lost touch with him after that. Much later, he'd gotten a letter from V. (he didn't recall the return address, if there had even been one). He hadn't replied. And, as I was anxious to know the substance of the missive, Lievel gave this unexpected (especially from him) and ambiguous answer:

"Abuse."

I didn't press him for details. We lapsed back into silence or what passed for it, that is to say, the sounds of water, which, with no one speaking, produced an impression of squalor and misery. Then Lievel was shepherding me back down the long hall previously described, where the lights had gone out. Until we reached the threshold, where we separated in the near-total confusion of our shadows, I saw no more of him than his stooped back: Should I consider this my final image of the man?

I was never to see Lievel again. I've reported our interview of that 7 May 19-- as faithfully as I could, being careful not to attribute any words to him but those I was absolutely certain he said, and taking pains not to invent the rest (which, for reasons that will become clear in time, would have been uncommonly easy for me). I want to emphasize that, even though I was to develop a sort of sympathy for the old man in the course of my coming journey, I was nonetheless in total disagreement with him when I left him that day. First of all, the infantile attachment to his dreadful baubles, the contrition of an artist who'd once shown such an appetite for life, had to my mind the flavor of things already said and already seen, regarding which I felt a very literary need for greater authenticity.

What was more, we really did have to take our leave of one another, and quickly, and with torn feelings, because Desiderio-Morelle had become, for one of us, such an object of disgust, and for the other (I say this thinking, in particular, of the painful dissatisfaction that followed my reading aloud) the very image of desire.

On emerging from the impasse E. des B., I remember a genuine sense of relief at finding a newsstand where, under the rain and in the light of the first streetlamps, I read the latest headlines of . . . Not because Lievel had converted me to his taste for vulgarity, but because it was still (*by contrast*, I should have said) an acceptable vulgarity. (This was around the time of the X. tragedy, one of those in which we only partly believe, and which the newspaper coverage turns into some kind of movement—of an exorcism, a dance, etc.— in which our own tranquility, as incredibly cynical as it may sound, is set in motion: becomes joy. I was so conscious of this that I even asked myself the question, as terrible as it was naive: Is it *morally right* that the awful disappearance of an eleven-year-old boy should evoke in me, primarily, a thirst for adventure?)

I dined that evening in a brasserie on rue ***. I probably had too much to drink. The thirst for adventure having become a thirst for words, I engaged my neighbor in table talk. For example, I aired my honest feelings on the X. case, and I think I shocked him. He made some reply to which I didn't listen, wrapped up as I was in my own thoughts. And I found myself talking about Lievel, without it ever for one instant occurring to me that my companion must have very little interest in the forgotten old writer and his bygone obsessions. As glass followed glass, I probably talked about myself. Primarily my childhood, I imagine, as tends to happen when the drinks are flowing, and even when they're not (but then we've all had that feeling of a deep friendship, a friendship stretching back into our boyhoods, when afterward we can't put so much as the semblance of a face on the person to whom we've lately poured out our soul: He loves me, but *who* loves me?). I couldn't even say which of us picked up the tab.

The next day, naturally, I laughed at myself for having felt the need to clear Lievel from my mind by such pathetic means, as if I were drowning my sorrows over an unattainable love or the incipient signs of old age. Since I had nothing more to do in Paris and the Desiderio mystery was still wholly unresolved, or nearly so, it was now he who became my source of freedom. I was reluctant to write a letter. I reasoned that the reply would come only in my absence, unless I included a vacation address and then stayed put—which would have tied me down. I decided to stop at V. along my way and took the first train. Could I really have done otherwise?

III

Such was the origin of the extraordinary journey whose tale I now begin. Little did I suspect, on that Sunday in the May of 19--, that it would take on such importance in an existence that was, by any standard, save for a few fatigue-related concerns, utterly untroubled. At the outset, of course, I'd planned on making only a brief detour through V. But we all know detours don't really exist. There are only royal roads. The reader will have to excuse such hackneyed fatalism, for it explains the quasi-maniacal scrupulousness with which I must here record certain details, certain impressions, *a priori* insignificant, of my arrival in V., which were first steps of the kind that cost so dear—developments will show exactly what their price was to be.

V. is what's known as a *ville d'art*, an official cultural heritage site. The approach by train is scenic. (I liked traveling by train because I could doze en route. In this way, I was able to sever my connection with Paris and make V., or O., or anyplace, an island unto itself.) I'd visited a lot of towns like V. with my mother, as a sort of bizarre compensation for my father's death, or perhaps an atonement for it. Instead of our warren of cramped maisonettes, each dirtier and more misshapen than the last, these towns were composed of neat, regular buildings and filled with sunlight. From a picturesque standpoint, they were a bit like what, in other families, would be the means of rekindling fond memories (and as a boy in history class, this was how I always naively interpreted Henry IV's famous remark on Paris): a Mass.

(Back then, I'd descend onto the platform just ahead of my mother and turn to take her suitcase from the train-car steps. Because I'd been thinking about it, I instinctively repeated the same action on my arrival that day in V., but instead of my mother behind me I found a passenger who, in my disappointment, seemed to me the very archetype of the stranger. He favored me with a look I'd describe as the polar opposite of the one I'd been hoping for—if *the opposite of my mother's look* can, in fact, have any intelligible meaning. And, since I'd already made a move to pick up this passenger's bag, I had to pretend to lose my balance in order to justify grabbing its handle—a gesture I still think might have been the expression of a genuine desire. But a desire for what? The passenger bore my words and actions with no apparent surprise.)

Under the influence of these memories (and no doubt my mother was traveling for no other reason than to relive memories of trips she herself had taken as a young bride—Florence, Naples, Syracuse—making mine the memories of memories—reality itself) my arrival in a sun-drenched city took on the character of an homage. Not that I observed any particular ceremony, of course, but in the absence of this, I took my time. I was the last straggler on the platform. I smoked a cigarette. I had a long look around the concourse—which wasn't worth the effort—as if it were an architectural rarity. I fiddled with the vending machines in the childish hope of reaping the benefits of someone else's negligence, haste, or

JEAN LAHOUGUE

an inexplicable blockage in the machinery—another flaw, in short. I stowed my suitcase in a luggage locker (though I'd had things stolen from them before, but what?—the usual changes of clothing, a toiletry kit of middling quality: I was experienced enough to be thoroughly blasé) in order to have my hands free.

I decided that a traveler who ran himself ragged trying to keep to a strict timetable was cheating himself of countless simple pleasures. I felt, as the last person to ascend the sunlit ramp leading to the town, that I was the richer for his acts of inattention. But I might have asked myself, because everything comes at a price: Would he, one day, begrudge me this?

V. sits on a slight rise at the edge of the L. plateau: what the geography books call a *tableland*, *mesa*, or (when the surface area is relatively modest, as in V., which has no more room to expand) a *witness butte*, one of those on which the marginal sea has left so many vestiges. The route I took from the station sloped upward between villas and gardens which one could only surmise, behind the thick walls that supported their balcony terraces, to be filled with flowers.

As I gained in altitude, the layout of this lovely town, which I knew exclusively, as I knew words in my early childhood, by hearsay, became clearer to me. Taken as a whole, it looked as if its architecture were progressively freeing itself from the accidents of the terrain (I was put in mind of the ambitious projects drafted by Boullée or Ledoux, both of whom drew inspiration from V.) in order to obey the lone imperative of a great desire. But no doubt

I, too, was full of desires (and now and then I would brush the walls unnecessarily with the tips of my free fingers, which were encumbered, but just barely, by Desiderio's manuscript alone) that manifested itself in various silly ways: thus, turning around and holding my hand out flat against the sun, I noticed that this hand now covered the entire railroad junction and station (so tiny that it seemed to be running only at the behest of the swarms of children looking down on it with interest from the ramparts)—until I felt a strange, disturbing absence, which I later understood to be that of my own exhaustion: despite the climb, I wasn't out of breath, I wasn't *dead*.

Within the town walls, the buildings were organized according to a beautiful, classical arrangement. The streets were warm. I felt an increasing sense of calm, and understood that it came from knowing that these houses were being wisely and lovingly preserved (when an architectural ornament deteriorated under the ravages of age or of the sea, which was less than ten kilometers away, it had to be replaced with a comparable new ornament, leaving its still-serviceable neighbors intact, so that the facades testified to both the march of time and a reassuring continuity). Silly as it may seem, I spent ten minutes in a bar-café, though I wasn't thirsty, just to penetrate one of these buildings.

V., I thought, was hardly the field of ruins I'd been expecting—influenced, no doubt, by my correspondent's pen name (this stubborn misconception dogged me still and reduced me to the supposition that I must be dealing with an *edifying* Desiderio-Barra, so to speak, when I was more interested in the destructive De Nome. I was almost glad of the mistake, thinking: I'll be free all the sooner!). The impoverished children who'd been born here must have left. Wealthy city-dwellers had moved in to replace them (between the two was a threatening period when people had had *to save*: this, no doubt, is when I should have come) because the houses were dream houses from which one could look down on the surrounding countryside from above.

And then I had a wild impulse: from the postcard rack on my left, I chose a panorama of V. (one of those that make you think: Where on earth was this shot taken from?) and slipped it, though not proud of myself for doing so, into my inside pocket.

Rue de Nazareth was on the opposite side of town. It was a bright street, practically unfrequented. *Nazareth* was a relic from the days of pilgrimages, to which many of V.'s streets owed their names borrowed from holy places. Number 11 was an unassuming house, but a tidy and pleasant one (Was I holding out one last hope for a ruin, which would have been very much an exception here? In this case, I'd have to say the preceding observation was a relief, and that I'd found a place that delivered), which appealed to me at first sight. It bore no resemblance at all to the villa I'd so variously described to my friends, and which, as a result, had become a composite—quite the contrary. I knocked several times. No one answered.

With that, I could have turned around and left V. But surely it was only natural for me to try and glean a little more information about my mystery man's possible stay. To tell the truth, I was ashamed of having come all this way for nothing (still harboring suspicions, however, that the whole thing had been a hoax). The emotional nature of my arrival had already faded from memory. We always pay dearly for forgetting our moments of enchantment . . .

Perhaps on some level I'd sensed the danger because I resorted to a kind of trick to absolve myself of apparent responsibility for what happened next. (The trick was one I'd invented, as have all children: when I knew I was in for imminent punishment, I'd mope around with a forlorn expression—taking care to keep mum on the causes of a transgression I'd be very hard-pressed to justify—until my mother, forgetting her anger and now seized with worry, would start talking and talking, saying fantastic, wonderful things to fill my silence.) Instead of knocking on a neighbor's door or asking at the shops I'd seen at the intersection, I stood there, arms dangling at my sides, in the middle of the pavement facing number 11. I assumed a blank, vacant expression, letting the sweater jacket I'd removed trail on the ground, the Desiderio manuscript—which made me no ordinary traveler—hanging from my other hand in place of a suitcase, as if I'd witnessed some indescribable cataclysm, trusting to what I knew of small towns and telling myself: Someone watching from behind one of these windows will eventually grow concerned and come out to talk to me—*it will no longer be my fault.*

(Foolish as it may seem, I remember counting to one hundred, the way one might do to pluck up one's courage—but courage for what?—so that all the beautiful things on the street that caught my eye—windows, verandas, etc.—were each stamped with a number—and for a long time afterward this number would pop into my head whenever I saw them again, or saw other things like them, turning the whole world into an itemized list . . .—the way, too, one might give another child [who could be named Desiderio, for example] time to hide.)

But to all appearances my calculations hadn't been far wrong: scarcely a minute had elapsed, in fact, before an old woman came to my aid.

JEAN LAHOUGUE

She hesitated—she must have been disappointed at not seeing anyone she recognized. But then again, she was frail and seemingly used to treading lightly. When she drew nearer and I got a better look at her face, I would have put her age at around eighty. I experienced a familiar uneasiness that often came over me in the presence of old women, made all the worse because this particular old woman had been conjured up by a bit of familial playacting that made me feel I was entitled to a very different reward (if my mother had lived, she would have been much younger than this woman, so my first reaction to her was: this woman is *still* alive, less from a sense of injustice than from sheer improbability), but the feeling quickly passed. She looked me over, paying particular attention to my hands, which were no longer as free as they had been a moment ago, but were caught (*in the act*, I might say) with a sweater jacket they were allowing to get dirty and the manuscript resembling a copybook.

"Are you looking for someone?" she asked.

"A distant relation. I was told he lived here. But the house seems to be vacant."

"Who might this relation be, monsieur?"

"Jean Morelle. But he could've been using a different name. He's an artist, you see . . ."

"I see . . ."

She added—was it an explanation?—that her son had a taste for the arts. She made me repeat the name. I spelled it. I said it was Morelle with a double L, E. I remember being happy to break down the names for her, as if I had all the time in the world (the weather was fine that evening on rue de Nazareth in V.). I was happy, too, to have told the little white lie regarding my purported family connection (really, I was simply sparing myself a labyrinthine truth) even while thinking: This is a sin!

In any case, the grandmotherly old woman had decided to talk. And what she said (which I heard in a state of mind—as I'm sure the reader will understand—that made it *music to my ears*) was to determine the course of my life for a long time to come. I sensed this importance dimly at best, without fully grasping it, because while listening to her, incredibly enough, I felt all the little pleasures described above swell to considerable proportions and—if this odd idea can be believed: become exhausting. But I thought: This is because I'm learning so much about Desiderio, far more than I did in an entire week of careful investigation, and because the times in one's life when one learns so much so quickly are rare and wonderful indeed, etc., and even: Haven't these truths sprung, just as in the old days, from my lies?

And yet it had all seemed so harmless and inconsequential at first!

Madame Vian, for that was her name, was the owner of number 11, that simple and charming house. (In the course of our chat, she'd suggested we go inside to *have chairs*—but I suspect it had more to do with pride than with sitting.) She herself lived in what she called an appurtenant building farther down the street, from which vantage point she'd seen me pass by.

She saw a lot of new faces pass by, as it happened. (The street was on the circuit laid out by the guidebooks for visitors who had a full day to devote to V.) Consequently, the first part of her discourse was nothing but a long, colorful procession of enthralled strangers.

One day, one of them had stopped in front of number 11, thinking it vacant and possibly for sale. The house had caught his eye because it seemed steeped in stories. He'd ended up renting it. Since then, other tenants had followed. It was in this way she'd come to know Morelle.

"I believe he was indeed your Morelle, monsieur: When he gave his name, it struck me that it was the name of a flower—my son had one, too, a long time ago, in the Resistance—but I couldn't say exactly which flower it was, on account of my memory … When you've got a head like mine, you really should write everything down!"

She added, in an undertone (and I was touched by the fact that she confided this guilty secret to a stranger—but it served equally as a friendly warning): "I didn't declare him."

Morelle or not, setting aside the question of his name, had proved to be a dream tenant for the old woman. He hadn't moved any furniture or changed the decor, as so often happens when people drive nails into the walls to hang up their own mementos or, unaccustomed to the new layout, overturn glasses, leave burn marks on the rugs, chip corners, etc. Above all, and I understood that this detail was key from hearing my interlocutor wax poetic about her dead son and the blissful years of her first marriage (which charmed me, because it was so in keeping with sweet, old-fashioned, familiar romances), he *knew how to listen.*

He must have taken a shine to V., where he seemed at liberty, his occupation being something in the literary line (which didn't take up much of his time, since he regularly left for long walks during the busiest hours of the day and then went out again in the evenings to the movies), and occasionally served as a tour guide—his landlady had known this—because he was well versed in the arts.

Nevertheless, one night he'd disappeared. He hadn't informed anyone of his plans. He'd seemed a shade sadder during his final week—could it have been a *matter of the heart*? Madame Vian had found the downstairs room, for the first time, in disorder: his suitcase and all his things scattered about, his papers torn up. She'd waited forty-eight hours before reporting the disappearance—since she'd been at fault for misfeasance—to one Sergeant L., a relative, not so much to recover the rent, which had been paid in advance (she mentioned the amount in passing, and I smiled because this was another sign), but rather out of concern and solicitude. That would have been ten days ago tonight. Could I, perhaps, shed some light on the matter, as a friend and relation?

As the woman spoke, she showed me around the house, and her game was clear. I played along because I was delighted to be enveloped in the smell of orange pomanders from my childhood. Besides, the void abruptly opened by Desiderio-Morelle, far from worrying me as it ought to have done, had literally sucked me in. I supposed the manuscript had been mailed from V. on the day he'd fled, hence the macabre but *a priori* reasonable hypothesis of a veiled attempt to justify a desperate act. I'd thought of this right away, yet without falling victim to the error it represented—for it was an error—: I'd taken, I thought, *too much pleasure* in my reading. And how could I accept that it was now this pleasure (rendered problematic by the distressing turn of events) that had unmistakably singled me out to resolve whatever tragedy this might be? I let myself be guided.

The ground floor comprised two huge, nearly square rooms with long, low furniture that somehow didn't look lost there. Its like had been made since time immemorial for women who were small and light and who traversed much greater distances than I did. And yet using it—to me, with my heavy, ponderous limbs—came easily to me. The tables had been recently waxed—although we still verified the fact by hand. There were flowers.

The wallpaper was embossed, and its repeating pattern of sprays, as I recall, with their thick outlines and shadows, looked like *cartapesta*: one wanted to touch them. The old woman's minor adjustments, straightening a pleat here, balancing the arrangement of a bouquet there, gave me, as if by tacit consent, permission to run my fingers over things as well.

On the second floor were two cozy bedrooms: Morelle's and another, unused, which was consequently called the guest bedroom. She'd put everything back in order. She added some additional order now, because things are never the dreamed-of ideal, and I felt an even more insistent need to put my own hand where hers had been, following in the tracks of this inordinate passion that made me wonder: To whom or to what is she martyring herself: Morelle, me, or some strange sensuality?

She opened the wardrobe where Morelle's laundry, washed and ironed ("Laundry service is included in the rent" she told me) was waiting for him. The suitcase had been stowed here, on the lower left, and she opened that for me, too, even though there was nothing particularly noteworthy inside except the care with which she had sought and found each item's exact place.

The pleasure I spoke of, nourished in this way with caresses, must have been plain to see. She herself was feeling a happiness that didn't shock me, even though it was understood that Morelle had become dear to us. Was it to justify this happiness to ourselves, or because she actually shared my confidence, that she suggested I tell *him*—because of course I would find him—that everything would be dutifully kept in readiness for his return?

How could I, then—thus appointed by both the woman and my own pleasure to search for the missing man—get back on the train for O., which in any case I'd already missed: it was late! I hadn't seen any hotels on my way, but I knew that the old woman had only one thing on her mind: to see me installed here, where the bed was already turned down. Hadn't she given me what might be called her terms?—and her preceding message could well have been the last of these.

I thought to myself that if I were going to conduct an investigation of sorts, there could be no better place for me than rue de Nazareth, where I could adopt Morelle's habits (with this somewhat foolish ulterior motive: that the repetition of the same actions would perhaps lead to a sympathy that might allow me to understand him). And this circumstance, which sealed the deal: There was a Utopias Museum in V. with landscapes by the real Desiderio, the one whose unorthodox history I'd been carrying around in my head for far too long: you see how the very laziness I felt about leaving that night was spurring me to *get started*.

And so I committed the folly, which seemed to me a necessity, of renting this house that had so pleased me from Madame Vian. (I scarcely bothered to remember that it was technically already occupied by a stranger who'd left behind his personal effects—with whom I said I'd come to an arrangement, taking the house with a devil-may-care attitude that was not at all like me.) And I handed my landlady a FF-- note. I had very little money on me: this, as they say, was all I could do.

(At that very moment, a somewhat curious phenomenon occurred which, even today, I'm at a loss to assign a clear significance or even its proper level of importance: As she reached out for the banknote, the woman first grasped me by the wrist with an effort that must have been extreme on her part, since the veins in her hand were extraordinarily distended, though I felt but little pressure. And I probably wouldn't even have noticed it if, realizing that the bill was going to fall to the floor, I hadn't looked down.) Then she took the money, and everything returned to normal.

The rest of my first conversation with the old woman (it was to precede many more) concerned, in part, her inexhaustible remembrances of her dead son, and in part the little details that would regulate my everyday life: water, heat, light. (She pressed the ceramic buttons that I had to press in turn—for the purpose of what unjustifiable verification?) She would do my laundry if I wished it. She would bring me fresh herbs from her garden.

On the other hand, she didn't tell me any more about Morelle that evening (and I myself forgot to ask her about *La Belle Dame*, for example, and any number of other issues raised by the manuscript) except to deplore the fact that the police had taken away the torn papers she'd reverently collected from all over the room. But by tearing them up, Morelle himself had designated them as unimportant.

I remember that the last thing she did, just before she left me on this final regret, was throw open the window (from which the view over V. was stunning as well as surprising, because the winding staircase led you to believe the town was behind you when really it was directly in front) in order to give the place an airing-out before nightfall. From then on, the window would belong to me.

When my landlady was gone, I stood there speechless for a long time, just as I'd done a short while ago, but to catch what, or whom? Faced with this undreamed-of new life to organize, and despite the woman's kind attentions (which I knew to be plentiful and hidden throughout the house: my Easter eggs), the bare manuscript of Desiderio's in my hand was a sorry thing indeed.

It must have been about half past six. I wasn't up for going back down to the station to collect my luggage, but figured I wouldn't really need it here. (Among other minor worries—I give the preceding one for whatever it's worth, and for the bitterness I feel at having made it the center of my concerns, even for a minute, at the moment I was entangling myself, inextricably, in this story—it made little difference whether or not I was clean-shaven the following day because, I thought indulgently, I owed myself a bit of neglect.) I brought back from the shop, which I'd seen further down the street, and which was, miraculously, open on Sunday, eggs, oranges, and wine.

For dinner I ate an enormous omelet and nearly all the oranges. I say this for the sheer joy of it: I had an incredible appetite. Also because I was overcome by my delightful sources of elation:

(That of finding, first of all, everything I needed at the very instant I realized I needed it—because my routine at *** in Paris had relieved me of all such concerns, I'd forgotten oil, salt, etc.: yet there they were, in the very cupboard where I thought they'd be—saved ten times over by the unfailing thoughtfulness of a desire that had anticipated mine—Morelle's, or the woman's?

That of recognizing, to some degree, the toy dinner set I'd used when having tea parties with a little neighbor girl named **— in which pinecones were sea urchins because we wanted them to be, and sand milk—and we said: What delicious refreshments, monsieur! . . . Quite so, madame!)

In consequence, I had grounds to wonder whether all the theories I would subsequently form regarding Morelle had their origins in this elation, or were nothing more than its offset, its counterweight. Could it be so, in truth?

I must have cut a ridiculous figure, shortly thereafter, as I sat in the bedroom in front of Morelle's open suitcase with all his things spread out on the bed. I was giving the most serious consideration to a couple of spare shirts (in good taste, I thought), a red scarf, a pair of leather dress shoes, a toiletry bag with a pocket mirror, hand towel, and washcloth—all of which took on an almost marvelous quality from the fact that I was examining them for signs of a possible adventure, repeating endlessly to myself that they constituted my *evidence*—but evidence of what?—and I handled them with infinite precaution, as if they were fragile in the extreme.

Much later, I put them back as they had been, managing to reproduce the woman's careful gestures, without having gleaned any additional insights into the missing man in the time between our two acts of solicitude. Then I went to bed. Naked. The night was singularly bright. I remember there was no hint of a trap (a trap recognized as such: it went without saying that I was allowing myself to be captivated, with pleasure, by happy, sentimental memories) apart from a tiny, transparent cobweb within arm's reach (and I was glad, because it was something the old woman had overlooked—the fault, at last, for which I'd probably been looking, unconsciously, ever since setting foot in the house—which made her comprehensible, or arrestable, if you will), near enough that I could intervene at any moment to save, or not—it was up to me—the insect held in thrall by the little orb-weaver. But—did I enter into the pleasure of the latter or the hell of the former?—I fell asleep.

IV

The morning of the first day came under the sign of the popular novel where the following words appear: "Those close to the inspector were continually surprised at his custom of immersing himself in the environment in order that he, who was nonetheless so different, might slip into the skin of the deceased," repeated cheerfully, because one sees things in an unexpected light when one wonders, somewhat stupidly, regarding an absolutely unremarkable object which one can either look at or not, touch or not, pick up or not: What would someone with nothing to do, do in this case?

I walked through V., whose shadows were all on the opposite side, still in that state of surprise in which I'd found myself on waking in the nude, which was not my custom. I said "*Bonjour, monsieur*" (or "*. . . madame*") to passersby, as one does in towns where their numbers don't make it impracticable. I drank milk at yesterday's café from a very commonplace glass, one of those in which one can read the most thoughts, if the saying is true that to drink from someone's glass is to know his mind. For I told myself, clasping it tightly between my palms, that the glass was V., naturally.

When I'd made a friend, or near-friend, of the server, for example, I inquired about Morelle. I sketched a thumbnail portrait of him (according to the fragmentary information provided by my landlady, whose descriptions, unfortunately, consisted chiefly of analogies: He looked like [insert name of friend unknown to me]).

I exhibited his red scarf. I said he might have been seen coming out of number 11, rue de Nazareth. But the fact that V. was a cultural heritage site with many people passing through made things difficult for my interlocutor.

Nevertheless, I made careful note of each place the missing man had been sighted, taking these reports with the grain of salt one would expect, and transferred them to a map I'd bought of V., in this way forming a kind of dotted-line profile of Morelle's habitual route through town, as well as others, hazier still, inscribed within it: that of a chance table companion, usually female, occasionally male.

(Wasn't I crafting, in my own way, behind all the environment-immersion mentioned above—while I was playing detective, obviously—something akin to a serious-minded police procedure, since my map was very properly divided into squares lettered A to L and numbered 1 to 12? This was a document that, though it didn't resemble anything, didn't even mean anything, at least gave me something to do with my hands: they were tingling with pins and needles, itching to invade the entire town.)

Then I, in turn, inscribed myself into the same circuit, which was far from disagreeable since it took me past all of V.'s most beautiful facades. It also went through lively squares: the one with fountains where there were swarms of children, the one with steps where men were playing pétanque (and *boules* thrown too far would roll right up to them, down which they would gradually, lumberingly bump step by step). I would have liked to join them.

JEAN LAHOUGUE

The place where I obtained the most definite information on Morelle was at a junk/souvenir shop across from the parvis of the town's principal church. I'd noticed it right away because, amid the sea of trashy objects, I knew there must have been a few real bargains, by means of which the curiosity I attributed to Morelle might well have been aroused.

I don't know what bizarre certainties, derived from twenty-odd pages, allowed me to envisage a man so fascinated by trinkets, provided these were of a caliber worthy of interest. (Imagine, around a crate of old deadbolt locks and hinges—I'm choosing, among many others, an example suited to this shop, which was packed with similar boxes of jumbled hardware and bric-a-brac—the stiff rosette of the doors they implied: one sees the sort of operations I was having the man go through, I who felt safe and secure.) Or this detail: Depending on the time of day and the angle at which one saw the shop window, the horrors within were, to a greater or lesser extent, cut into by the magnificent reflection of the parvis. In short, further signs . . .

(As I entered, a customer was debating the authenticity of some item or other with the manager, so that I had a chance to browse through the window displays full of old decor, every possible landscape, precarious piles of items such as might be seen in an attic [in the midst of which I discovered, as part of the same process—I mention this to explain the sort of awkward mental position in which I was about to find myself—a child engrossed in a re-edition of a book by Benjamin Rabier—probably someone's young relative on spring break—or a sleeping dog curled in a circle], butterflies preserved in amber, etc.)

When my turn came, I inquired about a vista of V. in cavalier projection, the kind reprinted in the old style, which are more legible than a Blay guide map, in truth simply to strike up a conversation that would lead onto the subject of Morelle. I was scarcely surprised—despite the number of out-of-towners who must come through the door—to learn that the man very clearly recalled the visitor in the scarf of whom I spoke.

This latter had struck him as a man of taste, someone who obviously knew his stuff when it came to art. The proof was the lithograph by **** he'd purchased, which the man affirmed was a rare find. Even so, there was still one of the series left, and he was kind enough to show it to me. Was it because of the awkward post-child position I mentioned? Or the certainty I'd gained of Morelle's having passed through this very place—whence the corollary certainty that everything I'd been told about him was true? Whatever the reason, I didn't for a moment suspect any chicanery on the shopkeeper's part, despite my astonishment, which this time was considerable:

The picture was an ordinary nude. I mean to say: a nude of deplorable conventionality, the likes of which Desiderio-Morelle, such as I imagined him, would never have admired. Meticulous, but without the craze for detail that can sometimes be captivating. The woman's eyes were closed, though less in pleasure than in sleep, as if this somnolence redeemed (?) the audacity of the exposed genitals (I want to emphasize that the aforementioned attraction to the ugly could in no way have been a factor here, given that the artist's line was good, the pose straightforward and unmannered, and no considerations of genteel prudery had entered in to awaken, through irony, the meager pleasures of scorn or naughtiness) I had no desire to touch.

And yet I didn't doubt that this image was indeed the one Morelle had selected. I don't even think I left it for later to find some droll resemblance or parallel apt to enhance the picture's value. I invented, with frightening facility, nonexistent reasons to like it. Then I bought it for an exorbitant sum, convinced I had come out ahead in the transaction.

The recto in which I obtained . . . did I say? of what verso?

It was only once outside that I felt I'd been had, for, even supposing the shopkeeper really did recognize Morelle from my description—which was unlikely—and really had sold him a drawing, how could he have passed up the opportunity to use my eagerness, which had so manifestly been eating me alive ever since my arrival in V., to foist some random piece of rubbish on me? (I'll admit I took out my acquisition then and there to examine it in the daylight, asking myself, quite literally, *Is this rubbish?*, which I didn't think the least bit odd until the unwelcome interest it was attracting from passersby made me roll it up again and tuck it under my arm.) I had half a mind to return to the shop, but I could picture the ensuing scene: the startled shopkeeper adamantly refusing to admit the truth, and, to top it off: throwing my own recent enthusiasm back in my face—it was unthinkable.

I decided, therefore, to go home to rue de Nazareth, taking the long way around in order to give myself time to put this reversal out of my mind, grazing the walls as before because the slight sensation of pain was helpful. (I remember that, at least initially, I dreaded a run-in with my landlady, as if it were a given that she'd insist on seeing the source of my distress. It seemed to me I would have been obliged on principle to show it to her, and doing so, I decided on some unconscious level, would have made me ashamed. Then, as the idea of shame began to intrigue me and my fear transform into an obscure hope, I suppose I tried to reproduce the conditions that would lead to me *finding* the old woman: loitering in the street, using the rolled-up picture as a telescope or a trumpet—and getting it dirty in the process—dragging my feet . . . all in vain.) Back in my room, the last traces of annoyance having dissipated, I drew up a battle plan of sorts.

I began with the topographical work already described, which offered me, within the quasi-circular perimeter of V., a distorted, but—all things considered—less vulgar drawing than the lithograph by Monsieur ****. After which, I wrote a summary of what I knew—without realizing that, here, too, my approach was preposterous: one always knows more—on the back of the map, with a morbid (fierce, childish) joy, because I felt like I was in a novel. Then (I think now that this great show of methodological rigor, on which the organization of my coming days was to depend, was perhaps nothing more than a natural reaction against the bitter disappointment of having let myself be hoodwinked a short while ago through excessive reverie) I tried, for the first time, to think through the situation clearly.

To start with, I held the identity of Morelle and Desiderio to be a settled fact, taking my pleasure in being here as what is commonly called a proof. Working from this premise, which I would not henceforth call into question, despite its tenuousness (and the mere fact of articulating its tenuousness would oblige me to conclude that the whole enterprise was founded—in theory, anyway—on a half-baked belief in some absurd metempsychosis) I formulated the following hypotheses:

In the first hypothesis, Desiderio was still alive. He'd left V. in haste, under some form of duress whose nature I had yet to ascertain. (I must, in the interest of truth, add this: The common habit of breaking down a problem into its component parts, the better to solve it, meant I saw the issue in naively simplistic terms: the nature of this duress was either *legal* or it wasn't. In the former case, I was thinking along the lines of, say, a violated residency restriction about to come to light—such situations were few and far between. In the latter, a whole panoply of mysterious forces suggested themselves to my imagination, and seduced me, I believe, with their aura of romantic glamor.)

In the second hypothesis, Desiderio was dead. I've already mentioned the reason I didn't think he'd committed suicide: my joy—which (reason or joy) is difficult to convey to others, I know, except through questions such as: Why would he, who was giving *me* the chance to live out the thrilling adventure I was currently experiencing in V., give *himself* only death? Or this, somewhat more petty because rooted in my concerns from before my trip: How could he round off (crown) his life with a text both so full of promise and nonetheless—I clung stubbornly to this shallow opinion—so *hastily dashed off*?

Another reason, which by the same stroke rendered the possibility of an accident implausible, confirmed my suspicions in a way that came to seem, in time, inexplicably ludicrous: *there was no body*.

I saved for last the third hypothesis, overly melodramatic in my view, of premeditated murder. And yet, however shocking the attitude may seem (owing, no doubt, to the fact that as a boy I had devoured so many crime novels that murder became, for me, fiction itself*—and in my mind I was saying *murder* rather than *crime* or *killing*, which must have sounded less apt to me, almost savoring the word), I believe this possibility held no horror for me. Am I forced, now, to suppose that it fascinated me? I simply judged, without alarm, without terror, that the circumstances made it conceivable. And even if I had been afraid...

So ended my preliminary analysis, from which—it goes without saying—I was able to draw no conclusions.

That same afternoon, I paid a visit to the police station. It wasn't a decision I made lightly, convinced as I was that in some of my hypothetical cases such a step would do Desiderio the greatest harm. But it seemed to follow a certain logic which words like *murder* imposed. It's likely, too, that I wanted the extraordinary things that were happening to me to be backed up by something official, and, I would even add: incontrovertible. If nothing else, I was determined to proceed with extreme caution.

The station, on rue du Temple, occupied a classical-style building that also served as the town courthouse. Having been designed for other uses, the interior left one with a disagreeable impression of the makeshift and provisional. Probably because it had been

....

* Since then, I've come to believe that this adolescent passion correlated with my own discovery of death. These novels were probably nothing more than a means of reducing death to its most meticulously rational causes, of justifying it, and, in short, of ritually, religiously negating it.

subdivided by partition walls into a warren of inordinately tall rooms with broken cornices. The human element, as they say—the people waiting, who seemed impossibly puny in comparison—was anecdotal.

I was shown to an office on the second floor, the building's original height having been split into only two. This was the smaller, but the window, in consequence, seemed enormous. Since it had no curtains, and since nothing could be seen on the other side but uniformly blue sky from top to bottom, one wanted to go closer and get at least a partial view of the street, but this was something visitors were apparently not authorized to do. The office was gray. Furnished like every other business office, with the addition of a calendar and a map of V. An ammonite, or Ammon's horn, which was the only decoration in evidence and which I was constantly tempted to pick up during the course of the interview, had been called into requisition as a paperweight.

The physical person of the police officer (I learned only later that he was one Inspector Morand) escapes me at present. I would put his age at around thirty. His face must not have had any features salient enough to impress themselves on my memory. And yet I'm certain this normality was subjective, in the sense that even the strangest face would become, for the person who owned it and saw it on a daily basis, a sort of norm in the long run. All I've retained, therefore, are its incidental expressions. Starting from this moment, I felt the lack of something as I stood before him: maybe this was it. Or this other absence: I had no gut reaction to him, either of hostility or sympathy.

I outlined out the motives for my visit with enough credibility not to expose myself to the risk of a summary denial, with the exception that I held back the mailing of the manuscript. This, I thought, was my ace in the hole.

"Sergeant L. told me about this case," he said.

After a slight hesitation, he added:

"Sergeant L. is on familiar terms with Madame Vian. She confided this story of the disappearance to him in his private capacity, and it was in his private capacity that he went to her house to check it out. The results were disappointing. Considering what I know about Madame Vian, I'll admit I was reluctant to open an investigation."

"And what you know about Madame Vian is . . ."

"Oh, nothing serious, don't worry. Let's just say she has an active imagination; you must've noticed that yourself. She lost her only son at the end of the war. I think she's been spinning a lot of yarns around him ever since. I didn't believe in this Morelle, for a couple of reasons: one, she seems to be the only person to have known or even seen him, and two, she describes him—according to L.—as being the same age and having the same personal habits as her son in '45. You said yourself you don't really know the guy . . ."

"He wrote me."

"Did you save the letter?"

"I destroyed it. But I can assure you it wasn't a figment of my imagination."

"And because of this one letter you came all the way from Paris?"

"I was planning to spend my vacation in V. anyway," I said, a little embarrassed. "He was asking my advice on a book . . ."

Then I quickly added, to change the subject:

"What about Morelle's things on rue de Nazareth? Madame Vian and I didn't dream those up!"

"Who's to say she didn't buy them herself? Shirts like the ones her son used to wear. Shoes in his size. Sacred relics in the cult she's built around him. It's not so unusual, you know . . . As for the letter . . ."

"The letter?" I urged him.

"I'm very sorry you destroyed it."

He looked at me.

It was hot. Behind me, typewriter sounds could be heard. Someone stuck his head through the door and saw that we were busy. Morand, on the subject of my letter, took on a tone that was just a shade pedantic, or perhaps mocking, and which became disconcerting after a while.

"Have you heard about the case of Anna D.?"

I said that I hadn't.* He started in on a very curious tale.

"Anna D.'s son," he said, "died in a concentration camp in the winter of '44. She emigrated to Palestine soon afterward, and from there she let it be known to various correspondents in Europe that her son was still living with her . . ."

"How does this story . . ."

"Just wait. All this wouldn't have been so strange if she hadn't sent her son's friends, *in his handwriting*, which she painstakingly reproduced, and under his name, letters so consistent with his usual trains of thought that not a single person caught on to the deception."

....
* In truth, I must have read an account of the case, together with a lengthy discussion by Professor A. H. Wögel, in the journal *Art et psychanalyse*. It had struck me because it resembled the extraordinary story of Lieutenant Kije. I had forgotten it.

He was still looking at me.

"When two of these friends turned up in Israel, she explained away his absence by saying he'd gone on a trip. One day they received, in her own handwriting, an announcement that ***—this was her son's name—had died in an accident. Shortly thereafter, they learned of Anna D.'s death, in J., on 19 July 19--."

"And you think," I broke in, "Madame Vian . . ."

"Is it such a stretch?"

I hesitated. I knew Morand was wrong, but my conviction was based on the Desiderio manuscript, which couldn't possibly be the old lady's handiwork, even supposing her capable of writing letters like Anna D.'s. There was also Lievel's testimony—at which I had no wish to point the finger. I settled for a laconic answer:

"I think it is."

He looked at me even more intently, and I thought it best to redirect the conversation a second time:

"Madame Vian mentioned some torn-up papers Sergeant L. had collected . . ."

He took his time before answering:

"I'm not bound by confidentiality regarding a case *that doesn't exist yet.* So . . ."

He went and selected from among a number of file folders one that appeared empty but that turned out to contain a reassembled jigsaw puzzle of two sheets of standard writing paper, which he handed to me.

"The police believe in being thorough," he said. "Sergeant L. spent an entire Sunday on this little game. He'll need a lot more Sundays to finish the rest."

I don't know if I successfully hid my disappointment from the inspector, who didn't take his eyes off me. I'd been expecting (probably owing to the word "papers") IDs, membership cards, documents with Morelle's photograph stapled to the upper corner (and doubtless I had come here primarily in search of that face). But I had little difficulty in recognizing a fragment of the Desiderio manuscript—a first or second draft: the mosaic aspect prevented me from being sure, and I didn't know the manuscript by heart, word for word—from which I learned nothing, except perhaps that Morand would soon be closing the gap (only a gap!) by which he still lagged behind me.

"What do you think?"

"I think," I said, by way of getting even for this letdown, "that an elderly woman who's probably never set foot outside of V. would have had a hard time coming up with this."

"Even if she used a model? She could've copied these phrases from a book. There're a lot of books out there . . ."

"The text as it stands would never have gotten published."

"But just suppose—this is another theory—suppose she found some of her son's scribblings and wanted to get them into print. She manages to type out the manuscript. She rips up all the sheets with typos—there are *bound* to be typos, she's never done this kind of thing before—and sends off the clean copy God-knows-where . . ."

As might be imagined, at this point I was closer than ever to losing my composure. Nevertheless, I had another conviction, one I hadn't articulated to myself until just then (having had no reason to do so) which concerned Desiderio's writing style in and of itself: I was clearly in a much better position than Morand to catch the many little details, winks, and allusions of varying degrees of intentionality, all of which led to one overwhelming conclusion:

"I can guarantee you," I said, ignoring the inspector's insinuation and gesturing at the jigsaw puzzle in front of us, "that this is a recent text!"

Morand looked at me for a long moment and then dropped his gaze to the ammonite, which I had an urge to take in my hands because it was, in truth, the best thing there, the most unwarranted.

"For the sake of argument," I said, "let's say for a minute that you agree with me: Morelle is not a figment of the old woman's imagination. He's really alive, or was alive. He left everything behind in his room in great disorder: his toiletry kit and all the rest—which Sergeant L. is trying to salvage (you have to wonder why, incidentally). What do you do?"

"I wait," said the inspector.

He looked at his watch and I understood that he was wrapping up the interview. Then:

"I wait. Everything happens in its own time. V. is a town with a lot of people passing through. During the season—the high season!—I get reports of disappearances like this, real or imagined, on a daily basis. Sometimes we find a body washed up on the beach. Sometimes we don't. In which case, there's every chance the trail will go cold and stay that way. So I'll wait for my body. But while I'm waiting, I'll tell you right now, I'm not going to go dragging the ocean!"

He stood up and steered me to the door with a hand on my shoulder. It was then that, indicating the endless expanse of sky outside his window, he concluded his speech with words that were so formulaic, so heavily loaded with melodramatic menace, that I had to smile:

"It's a beautiful day. If I were you, I'd enjoy my vacation. You don't want to enter into these awful stories."

Was this naivete? And, if so, was it his, or mine?

Such was the substance, down to the smallest details my memory has cast up, of my first interview with Inspector Morand. I was, to tell the truth, somewhat shaken. The confidence with which he attributed to the woman I'd come to mentally call *the grandmother* a sort of Machiavellian devotion (and I was thinking of her face, of the word she was often unable to find—and in place of which she'd straighten, for example, a painting that was hanging askew, or fondle some object) seemed to me unjustifiable.

And yet the inspector's arguments were sound. The perspicacity with which he'd sized me up had given all his reasoning the stamp of logic, however strong my own opposing convictions. As for his final warning, it had felt like one of those of events that suddenly slip the bonds of the cozy, rational universe where we feel at home, events that are supernumerary, that come from elsewhere, that *are* elsewhere. The ones we must have imagined.

On the other hand, the rigor and skepticism Morand had evinced didn't seem to me sufficient for solving what I had christened, with childish smugness, *the Desiderio case*. Though I myself was capable of little more than intuitive impulses (would I say, again, that this was a question of taste?), I consoled myself with the thought that I was better equipped than he.

While I was turning over such ideas, I hesitated—unconsciously, it would seem—to return to rue de Nazareth directly. I might have run into Madame Vian, and I suppose this eventuality seemed less than desirable, as if my landlady had become Doubt itself, or some confused expression of the impossible (I mean to say: in the way that a word or object on which we've focused our attention to an unusual degree, or in an unusual way, can sometimes become, for a split second, imbued with a radical implausibility, only to return, a split second later—and just as inexplicably—to *normal*). Tomorrow, I thought, these contradictory images would no longer haunt me, and I'd be able to give her an honest look.

(I recall that I arrived, in the course of this hesitation, at the square with the steps, now abandoned by the pétanque players. I found myself in the middle of the pitch, my hands aching to hold a weighty pétanque *boule*, for the sense of reality I imagined it would provide—a bit like the pinch people ask for to help them believe in the same—when I saw a stranger approaching me: I'd forgotten that loitering around like this empty-handed, especially for an extended time, tended to attract such characters. But he didn't ask me what I was doing there. He begged my pardon and handed me a piece of paper that, according to him, I had dropped. It was the rough outline in which I'd made a very serious attempt to take stock of my investigation, and which must have fallen from my pocket when I'd pulled out my cigarettes. I stammered my thanks. I couldn't bear to look directly at the man, certain that he had read the document and had formed an entirely wrong idea about me as a result. The paper in my hand was the exact opposite of a dense, round mass.)

I hung around the shopkeepers for a while in the vague hope that, where I'd randomly dropped Morelle's name and given his description, tongues would have been loosened since that morning. I was waiting for someone to bring up the subject on his own, but as I was simultaneously doing my evening's food shopping, the only responses I received were prices.

It was late when I got back to number 11. My legs ached from so much walking around V., and I lay down.

(Here a silly little incident occurred: Hardly had I stretched out on the bed when, from the longed-for softness, emerged the sound of crumpling paper. It was none other than the **** lithograph. In order to keep Madame Vian from finding it—we had agreed that she would come by to do my housekeeping, and in fact she had come by, since there were fresh flowers—I'd hidden the print by laying it flat between the sheets. When I pulled it out, the lady, as might be expected, was not a pretty sight . . .)

I simultaneously thought of Anna D. (whom I endowed with my landlady's innocent features, and from that moment on I was unable to believe in her adventure: it was nothing more than a pretty story told me in the hopes of lulling me to sleep), reproached myself for the scrapes (worthy of a child who was torn between causing mischief and going on a treasure hunt) I'd unwittingly gotten myself into—and, perhaps in a spirit of defiance, doubled down.

This was how I wound up spending the whole evening in front of that vulgar nude. I even indulged in a kind of primitive vandalism (to the point that I'm left wondering, today, appalled at so much unjust animosity, whether Monsieur ****'s drawing didn't have more to recommend it than my summary judgment had discerned): accentuating the creases that subdivided it, first in pencil and then, irreversibly, in ballpoint pen and various other pigments that came to hand during my lazy meal—egg yolk, wine, orange juice, etc.—and gradually made this nude into an unspeakable caricature, a running sore of colors that I spent a good while tearing with the tip of every sharp thing I could find. After which—was I finally breaking free of childish things by ritually destroying, one fine evening, the obscene image that had often aided me when I touched myself? from now on my women would be real women—I burned it in the hearth.

I remember that an unpleasant smell of charring lingered in the house for a long time afterward, despite the window being cracked.

V

The following days found me in a markedly different frame of mind. I don't know but that the naive auto-da-fé I described, while unburdening me of a certain measure of shame, hadn't also stripped me of my enthusiasm and curiosity. The fact remains that I scarcely believed anymore in the extraordinary adventure, the promise of which, for a brief instant, a confluence of singular circumstances and feelings had dangled so tantalizingly before my eyes. Henceforth I would no longer play detective—for decidedly it could be nothing but a game—except to prolong a pleasurable stir of emotions. Each passing hour further persuaded me that this was an artificial pose, and that I would soon be reduced to a mere vacationer.

First, there was the undeniable fact that no one in V. had retained a conclusive mental image of Morelle, my landlady and the souvenir seller excepted. In the latter's case, my belief that for him it had simply been an opportunity to make a quick sale was now unshakable. As for Madame Vian, who had taken to coming over for a chat in the evenings, she practically never mentioned her former tenant anymore. As often happens in older people, distant memories took precedence over recent events. And so the lost son, as if to confirm the inspector's theories, gradually pushed Morelle into the background, nay, into fiction.

It wasn't that no satisfactory answers would be given to my questions (on the contrary, it seemed clear that if Madame Vian felt, for example, a love every bit as fanatical as Anna D.'s, she was, by contrast, altogether incapable of turning it into any sort of imposture).

In this regard I admit, not without shame, that I laid a number of traps for the elderly lady, such as slipping in, during the course of a conversation, the odd direct allusion—a quotation, the retelling of an anecdote with only the slightest warping—to the Desiderio manuscript, only to observe in her, each time, the most sincere incomprehension, to my great embarrassment.

But these questions themselves had lost, under the effect of small pleasures and successive obliterations, much of their relevance. Besides, they were gradually assuming the shape—this was already making me smile—of those academic formulations found in old-fashioned metaphysics: "Where did the man come from?", "What was his purpose in V.?", "Where did he go after his disappearance?"—was it really necessary to answer?

And so it was by a sort of inertia that I continued the plan I'd drawn up for myself, namely, for a start: to make the rounds of all the local haberdashers, leather-goods shops, and shoemakers with Morelle's effects. They seemed to me expensive and well made, the kind of things that wouldn't be sold in such quantities of identical units that merchants wouldn't mark the day of each sale with a white stone. Though I had little hope of anyone remembering the purchaser, I thought I might at least discover whether or not they had ever carried such articles.

(Speaking of these articles, I recall that at first I left number 11 with only the shoes, inexpertly wrapped in paper. I hadn't gone three steps before the idea of strolling through V. holding these shoes, as if I were trying to avoid waking people, struck me as so ridiculous that I immediately doubled back to the house. It was then that I decided to put all Morelle's things back in his suitcase and go out with that, which was, at any rate, less bizarre.)

I pretended I wanted to buy shoes, a suitcase, and shirts of the same design (this wasn't altogether untrue, for I greatly admired all of them) but I was told at every shop, unanimously, that the brands were quite rare—probably only to be found in Paris.

Which didn't prove much of anything.

The fruitlessness of my efforts—these were now no more than half-hearted attempts at inquiry, and the traveling case of Morelle's I was carrying around had become so familiar to me that it had lost its power of fascination, like a ten-day-old toy—would have quickly driven me to throw in the towel had not a new development soon arrested my attention.

It all began with the indescribable sensation of a presence around me, or rather with the curious and complete absence of any feeling of tedium, whereas at such a moment—when I'd lost nearly all interest in the present venture and had not as yet undertaken any work on my Desiderio book, the real one this time—an extreme weariness would have seemed more natural. (And I told myself, absurdly, that my happiness wasn't happiness!)

At the outset, I credited this well-being to Madame Vian, whose unflagging solicitude never ceased to move me (and she was bringing me still more flowers, about which I wondered—after walking the length and breadth of V. and seeing, ultimately, very few gardens, and those filled chiefly, despite the season, owing to what interminable winter? with little labels: poppy, amaryllis, which were nothing but the promises of flowers—: Where are they coming from?). But even away from her presence the feeling persisted, with little alteration, that I was of interest to someone, with all that this implied of vanity and agreeable self-consciousness. And so I was sure I was being followed.

One evening, while crossing the fountain square (as I'll call it because I've forgotten its actual name), the flight of a departing swarm of children, bringing with it a sudden and unexpected calm, revealed to me by the same stroke a footfall some dozen meters behind me, which someone hadn't had time to muffle.

I turned and saw a small, bespectacled man of indeterminate age, goggling at me—which is all I can remember, so odd was the impression—in a cartoonish fashion. No doubt caught off-guard, the man stopped short and applied himself to the examination of a facade on the square. I can see him still, pulling his glasses onto his nose to decipher the inscriptions consisting of Roman letters and various interlaces—for he was fortunate (I say fortunate, convinced as I am that he was improvising a pretext for himself) that nearly everywhere in V. there were architectural exemplars to justify such pauses. I could think of nothing to say to him and continued on my way.

On another occasion, I was walking beside the ramparts on rue ***, where their height is noticeably lower. On an impulse, I hoisted myself up on some projecting stones, intending to peer over the top and thereby get a view of the country below.

But instead of the country below, what I discovered was the countenance of a man (without glasses. I'm not sure it was the same man as before: I would have had to see him standing up, and for a longer time) comfortably niched in the embrasure with his back, curiously, to the panorama.

JEAN LAHOUGUE

My surprise nearly toppled me off the wall (as if some artless assault had been repulsed by this lone, anodyne visage?). But I couldn't help reflecting, afterward, that a lookout post such as this would have been ideal for observing my movements across a range of at least three hundred meters.

These were not isolated incidents. Nevertheless, most of the time the hustle and bustle of the street served to make the surveillance less flagrant. When I happened to feel the weight of a stare at such times, it was impossible to pinpoint its origin with any certainty. I was always surrounded by gawkers, tourists with their telltale brochures in hand, the very picture of innocence, and there was never any figure I could have identified through cross-checking as being the same person: it was evident that my shadower, if shadower there was (and the idea still struck me as rather fanciful), took care to vary his appearance from day to day.

The funny thing was that this tailing, far from being intolerable, delighted me, at least in the beginning, owing to its aura of mystery, I suppose. (There was also my recollection that, as an only child playing by myself, I used to require, for each of my solitary acts—whether I considered them to fall within the realm of good or, more imperatively still, within the realm of evil—a sort of spectator and judge whom it seemed logical for me to call God the Father. It was not impossible that I might have been nostalgic for such voluptuous persecutions, and I wondered, on the subject of this voluptuousness: Was my shadower judging it?) At worst, then, it might happen that, walking down a street of great architectural unity sandwiched between Desiderio and this other, each elusive in his own way, I'd feel a vague unease, but one so fleeting that I'd already be thinking better of it.

(I recall, in connection with this, a more or less analogous situation that will perhaps give a better account of cherished, vertiginous moments such as these. A few years earlier, I happened to be driving through a pine forest. I was behind the wheel of a car then in mid-volume production, white, and immensely popular at the time. The road was perfectly straight, and I had doubtless drifted off into my usual daydreams when I suddenly noticed that I was between two cars identical to my own in every respect. Their speed, too, matched mine, so that the intervals between us, which were equal, remained constant. Whereupon I was violently seized by the feeling that I was moving—between the rear and the front of a single, unique vehicle that could only be my own, seen from without in infinite series—*through an inconceivable space*. Then the equilibrium, the two cars having turned off the road or a village having come into view, was broken. Was I left, then as in V., with the memory of anxiety, or of pleasure?)

I hardly stopped to wonder—so much was I letting myself be carried along by these surprises—who was spying on me and for what reasons, I who knew nothing, who was finding nothing, who would have already reverted to a tourist as enchanted as the rest if not for this. One of Morand's men, possibly? Without giving it any further thought, I simply stuck with what had been my original plan: when, having finished making the rounds of the shops, I was faced with the dual necessities of trying a different approach and of clearing up the mystery of my chaperone, I went to pay a visit to the Utopias Museum.

On the one hand, both Desiderio and the book I had inside me were calling me thither—I'd often told myself it was my main reason for coming to V. On the other hand, I thought it would be an adroit move on my part to confound my shadower by making a decisive break with custom and going to *a place where there would be no one*—I knew this from my experience of provincial museums—or at least where every presence would be so deliberately intentional that the petty motives I ascribed to this man would have—should have—, I concluded at the end of some chain of reasoning, stuck out like a sore thumb.

It is quite inconceivable, now, to think that such momentous progress, both in the apprehension of the truth and in my life itself, could have been born from so much indolence and error!

(This is not the place for a meticulous, faithful account of the Utopias Museum in V. Let it suffice for me to summarize a few of its features in order that the reader might have a more concrete understanding, if not of Desiderio-Morelle [who had gone there, I'm certain, had molded himself, formed himself there, and it was this changed man that would thenceforth be important for me to come to know], then at least of the idea I was later able to form of him.*

....

* For the rest, please refer to J. H. Vael's fine book, to the inventory housed in the museum archives as document 10 AS, etc. Cf. the bibliography graciously provided in the reception area of the museum itself, at the entrance to the chapter house belonging to the former bishops (though it can easily be found elsewhere), among a few essential images, some slides that would have to be looked at in the light, a map, a brief commentary.

It is worth noting, for instance, that a naive concern for order—or else the constraints of the building itself—has caused V.'s museum, reception area excluded, to be divided into four sections [fairly arbitrary ones at that, with the apparent omission, among others, of utopias of pure art, by which I mean: architectures born of strictly aesthetic necessities, of the painter's or drafts-man's materials themselves, of an initial curve that entails future arcades . . .—but all the utopias in the collection incorporate, more or less consciously, more or less sporadically, such concerns. Also, utopias of the past—golden ages, Edens—but, outside of time, the past . . .] namely:

The first section is dedicated to philosophical utopias: designs for cities of dizzying rationality in cavalier projection: nothing shrinks toward the horizon. But there are also incredibly detailed maps [most often inscribed within circles, squares, or stars] and, even more real, more credible: scale models—one can, but mustn't, touch. Complex wheeled assemblies make these cities turn, but there is no comprehending under the action of what wind, what river, or then again: what time. This is not for lack of commentaries or learned references [complete with supporting citations], however, for everything here manifests a desire to be perfectly understood. What is clear is that these walls will shape the passions.* And I remember smiling at this idea.

The utopias in the second section lie on the far side of some cataclysm, carved out by it [and not, in this instance, by man] or by time [but a time whose oddly selective erosion has obliterated vast swaths and preserved tiny flourishes, the same as when a person

....
* As attested to by Cabet's prudish and naive remark in the margin of one
  picture, that in such cities adulterers would find no refuge, or, *a contrario*,
  this remark of Fourier's: "I am discovering God's plan."

remembers]. From another perspective, they might also be cities of which not all is told: they would thus be ruins by omission. The few isolated people traversing them,* faceless and functionless, are merely fleeing, because the object, seemingly, is a bare landscape of implausible equilibria. But explanations are sparse. Justifications, too: At most, one can ask whether classifying these works as utopias might not reveal a flawed appreciation of them. It will of course be understood that this was Desiderio's room.

The third section concerns oneiric utopias. Here [?], the here-after is *not* after, it exists in a parallel present. A little inattention or a different kind of attention: You're already there. The cities are cobbled out of everyday objects put to willfully perverse uses, out of fruits, flowers, or bodies. It's not uncommon to find, in a place where at first one thinks one is looking at something rather cold, the petrified curve of an arch, for example: the small of a back. There is nothing but the erotic in these Oikemas, the *tempietto* and the stele, but, let it be said with a straight face, one realizes this only at length: Initially, one is simply happy; when one finally under-stands why, it's too late.

The final section of V.'s Utopias Museum is devoted to New Jerusalems, which one reaches at the end of labyrinthine itineraries, paths of both travail and glory. One plainly sees, from their ideal-ized features, that all the men are Christs and all the women Marys, and the setting is the world when it was young [in that the cities there remain new for all eternity] on a Sunday.

From here, a gallery leads back to the point of departure. In this gallery very simple, anonymous portraits are on display, about which one wonders [having gotten into the habit of unraveling a mystery of extravagant intentions at every turn]: Where's the

....
* Added later, according to de Dominici, by Belisario the Albanian.

utopia? And, in fact, one is so surprised at this simplicity that one remains persuaded for a long time that it must be some sort of enigma. [But in all likelihood these are only charitable donations—or else withdrawn from the collection because they didn't fit in—and were stored here for lack of a better alternative.] After which, one either gets a souvenir or one doesn't, and one leaves.)

On the day I visited V.'s museum for the first time, the layout was appreciably different, to my great disappointment, in that the entire Desiderio collection had been sent out for use in temporary exhibitions, some to the National Gallery (such was the case, notably, for *Vision of the World's End*), some to the Museum of Gothenburg (*City in Ruins*, etc.).

A brief explanation was stapled to each panel, along the lines of: "Normally on display here is—the title—by Monsù Desiderio (?–?), 17th century. This painting is currently away on loan in—the city—," illustrated with a photograph, smaller than life and necessarily a rough approximation of the absent work, to give some idea of it notwithstanding.

In place of the hoped-for *pittura metafisica* were hung portraits borrowed from the gallery described above, or from a common fund, views of V. by God-knows-what Sunday painter (creating the following strange impression: the ruins whose pale reproductions one saw in vignette were so *solid* by comparison that the intact streets and facings were nothing but the ruins of those ruins): disappointment itself.

Incidentally, disappointment of another order awaited me in the course of my visit (whatever recompense there may have been in the pleasure of exploring the other rooms): I'd thought to draw my shadower out of the crowd by dragging him into this deserted place, not so much to call him to account as in the hope of finally *getting a good look at him*. But no other visitor entered on my heels, no one—I verified this through the windows—seemed to be posted outside, and I began to think that, despite the aforementioned beauties, I'd come here for nothing twice over.

(To be fair, there was someone spying on me a little, but it was the apathetic museum guard—apparently the same one who exists in every museum, and who was endowed with the customary sorcery. He looked at me looking at things, and when, abandoning these things, I looked at him in turn, he would no longer be looking at anything, according to a kind of absurd jacquemart of our respective curiosities—what, then, were the things themselves curious about? It wasn't until later that I would come to be intrigued by this man.)

In any case, I spent more time than was necessary (if there was such a thing as a necessary amount of time) on my visit, partly to spite the guard who was in every doorway, partly because I was relishing this possibility, which made all of this *a fortiori* desirable: to deliberately take down one of these utopias from the wall as he watched and walk out with it. And so I started thinking, how far would I go (but the vision of Morand, with whom I might have to contend, dissuaded me)?

I finally made my way toward the exit, and it was there—as if all the hopes of which I'd been dispossessed had taken on an original, tangible form outside of myself—that the day's landmark event occurred.

There was, in the middle of the reception area that had to be recrossed—in the wrong direction, one might say—in order to leave, a table covered with maps, postcards, slides, and monographs. Since I wanted to get some reproductions, I addressed myself to the young woman standing behind it, who was pretty and, if I can permit myself to explain my misapprehension by this naive judgment, altogether in the spirit of a painting (I mean to say: not immediately, not overwhelmingly desirable, because giving, at first glance, the impression of inaccessibility. And now that I think of it, this was probably, in all stupidity, only because she was on the opposite side of the table where things were being sold. Otherwise . . .). From the look she gave me, I could tell something abnormal had occurred.

In truth, she was a visitor, and she herself, seeing me approach the table whose central location was deceptive, had taken me for the person in charge of the goods on display: she'd been about to ask me for the same reproductions, perhaps, when I'd spoken first.

The strangest part is that we were more abashed than amused by the misunderstanding, and after exchanging hasty explanations (even if it means I must be judged a prize fool for not finding the words to make her stay a moment, to make her laugh if nothing else), I allowed her to disappear into the museum.

I myself judged this conduct ridiculous, but, in my defense (this, at least, is the reason I hit on to excuse both my imbecility and the high-school-student behavior that was to follow), I owe it to myself to say this: Something had disconcerted me, and that something was not just the woman's body but also an echo, a *sign*, which I recognized as having its origin in Desiderio's manuscript. It wasn't set in a museum, and the details of the episode—when I double-checked—were entirely different. Yet the fact remains that the encounter with the famous *Belle Dame* had happened in more or less congruent circumstances, around a table where I-know-not-what sale was to take place. I repeat: These vague analogies were evidently no more than an excuse—on the one hand. On the other: a pretext for an attempt, worthy of an adolescent, to make good somehow (I hoped). Let the reader be the judge:

To begin with, I decided it would be oafish to await the young woman's departure in the middle of the reception area, where my presence, for a solid hour if she were as enthralled as I was, would not be justified in either her eyes or those of the guard, who was once again standing in a nearby doorway. By contrast, I thought the deft move would be to take up a post outside, at a café terrace, for example, where I'd have all the time I needed to come up with a joke, the one I hadn't made a moment ago—all sins erased.

But there was no café along this street, unfortunately, nor any store whose grid of aisles I could have patrolled to pass the time, nor any other place where it would have been excusable to pace in circles. The lone refuge was a telephone booth on the opposite sidewalk, in which it would be apparently as uncomfortable as it would be absurd to wait for such a long time. I therefore twice (which seemed to me the limit beyond which people would start to wonder about me) walked the length of this street where one could do nothing but pass through, at a speed I hoped was *normal*, before resolving to enter the booth and bear my misfortune in patience.

(Of course this was all quite juvenile, and one can readily imagine that it is not without a pang of shame that I describe the circumstances of this interminable lying-in-wait for an unknown woman I told myself I didn't desire—for what reason? In particular, I recall the lady who came to make a phone call, whom I made wait in vain for such a long time: and it was *I* who resented *her* for watching my lips, thanks to which I had to mime a conversation into the receiver, answering the void with every fool thing that came into my head, the subjects being the *Belle Dame*, utopias, which squares in V. were livelier than others, and I don't remember what else, until, exasperated, she finally decided to come back later . . .)

When at last I sensed that I really was wasting my time, I returned to the museum on an idiotic pretext (I had ostensibly lost an important paper, for the sake of which I was allowed to make another tour of the rooms—all deserted): the unknown woman was no longer there.

And my stakeout, and her mysterious disappearance, making her suddenly dear to me, even incredibly so, I dared to interrogate the guard—who gave the impression of appalling laxity. There was a second exit, through the little garden of the chapter house and the lapidary museum.

Such were the vicissitudes (but the most naive element of the adventure was probably to have ever felt shame about it) of this first encounter with Vanessa C.—because that was her name, as I was to learn so soon and so well. The reader will readily conceive how inattentive I was that evening to my conversation with Madame Vian.

In truth, I had a gift for appearing to listen to people, for instinctively nodding when necessary—and I never knew why it was necessary—for looking them full in the face, seeing only what I wanted to see, in this case the unknown woman, my main recollection of V.'s Utopias Museum. (Furthermore, while the old woman was repeating herself, I felt the need to *verify* in the manuscript . . .

JEAN LAHOUGUE

what, in fact? that a barely convincing similarity gave me official license to covet an unknown woman? And Madame Vian rushed through her reminiscences because she misinterpreted my impatience . . .)

Then something struck me in the words that until that moment I had been hearing as mere melody, something that preempted Vanessa C., was too caricatured, for example, for me to daydream through, like the story of her faithless husband that my landlady tried to cast as high tragedy ("He tells me he's going out for cigarettes. He walks out the back door, the one leading into the little courtyard, I remember it like it was yesterday. *Monsieur!* He never returned again!"), but which was in reality so comically prosaic that I had trouble keeping a straight face. And I was brought down to earth by the fact that I found it unbelievable.

Then I tried to steer Madame Vian's confidences toward my own preoccupations, toward Desiderio, the *Belle Dame*, and, to begin with: Did Morelle *keep company* (this was the vocabulary of my interlocutor, who also said *marriages* for *mixtures*) in V.?

"I believe so. I seem to have it in my head that I must have seen him with a young woman from time to time."

"What did she look like?"

But she looked like all the young women of today. So that, taken aback as I was by this general confusion suggesting to my mind endless parades of beautiful women, all exactly alike because all young, what could I have said?

Madame Vian was already moving on to the young women of 19--, where I was no longer following her, and I, without ceasing to look at her, saw the unknown woman from the museum telling me she had nothing to sell me and for good reason, and finally flitting off to the Fourier-Cabet-etc. room, leaving me stupefied—Madame

Vian speaking very gently from this point on because she took this stupefaction to apply to her.

A little later, picking up on her son's name, I asked (this was, with the provocation, the indelicacy, the cynicism mentioned above, in order to try one last time to make Madame Vian into another Anna D., because it would have been a convenient solution, impelled by God-knows-what necessity that I myself deemed, even as I formulated the suggestion, abominable):

"What if your son should come back one day, to this very place . . . ?"

To which she gave—pitiless herself, and mad, too, in her own way that was not Anna D.'s, in which what is called the wisdom of nations was overturned—this singular reply:

"He would be an old man, monsieur. At least he entered into history young . . ."

And me again: Was I hell-bent on distracting myself from my love, or what?

"Are you quite sure, Madame Vian, that your son is dead?"

". . . I *touched* him . . ."

VI

I hadn't forgotten about Vanessa C.—whom I wasn't yet calling by this name—but V., which couldn't have exceeded two thousand souls in the off-season, nonetheless seemed to me far too large to ever permit of finding one woman.

I believed the roads straight, but they bent imperceptibly in sympathy with the line of the ramparts: I couldn't see to the end of them. I was never where I thought I was, and when heading, or so I supposed, directly toward the fountain square, for example, I would be surprised to find it a little to my left—judging by the children's cries. Wasn't I also holding to a line of reasoning of a sort, when I made an exterior circuit of town as if to get a better grasp on it, all those who were eluding me having—I was seeing to this!—fewer chances of escape—from what, incidentally?

(In truth, I was giving myself as pretext the fossil rocks of the mesa, where I hoped to make a discovery comparable to Morand's—regarding which it will be remembered I'd felt a certain jealousy. And I more or less told myself that if I brought back an ammonite more beautiful than the inspector's, it would be tangible proof of a competence nigh unlimited in scope . . .)

What I didn't know was that what I was experiencing, just then, was the moment of precious equilibrium in which Desiderio, the mystery woman, the shadower (whom I was still seeing everywhere, but far too much to assign him any features) were still blended together in what can only be called a desire—my buzzardlike circles being a manifest sign that I was the one doing the hunting. Because initially I was curious (what I mean is: indiscriminately curious about art, my persecutor, and Vanessa's body), the object of this passion coming into focus only at length.

For Vanessa C. was to become my mistress. Why not say so *avant la lettre*? Wasn't I starting, with altogether clumsy gestures— given the talus and the tilting streets—, uncovering little by little, then casting off, the passersby, the children, the houses, the habits that hid her from me for so brief a time, to undress her? Every step taken is a shirt torn.

I recall that, one evening, convinced someone was watching me, I wheeled around to discover a lovely white facade that a bend in the road had previously hidden from my view. The lone person in sight, whose back was to me, was studying it attentively (he couldn't have anticipated my movement. From which I concluded that he must have been absorbed in his contemplation for some time, and that I'd been mistaken: no one had been paying any attention to me). Then the man reached out and caressed, twice, the beautiful molding around a window. I was unaware at the time why such a gesture stirred me so, but didn't everything that had been revealed to me represent a small step toward the nudity of a body?

The circumstances of this second encounter with Vanessa C. owed just as much to chance accidents and novelistic fancifulness as on the day of the utopias. Nevertheless, they do warrant a few explanations.

JEAN LAHOUGUE

To start with, the aforementioned analogies, even the forced ones, between the *Belle Dame*'s intrusion and the scene in the reception area, did not fail to intrigue me. Owing either to this, or else a to general tendency to let myself be guided by *urges* (if I ever suspected what is commonly called the wheel of fate behind this affair, I must acknowledge that it was being turned by a multitude of tiny acts of surrender to which I never would have stooped on rue de H.) into carrying out puerile experiments—such as erasing a chalk arrow in order to disorient the swarms of children following I-know-not-what treasure hunt, etc.—, there was gaining ground in me—conversely, I should say—an outlandish idea.

Given that one episode from Desiderio's manuscript had been substantially reproduced by chance, why shouldn't I, in turn, induce the conditions favorable to repeating another ordinary episode from said manuscript? I'll admit that such an undertaking, though enchanting to the dreamer, seemed like a dead end to the seeker I had become (marked by an attitude of blinkered seriousness). Even so, with no useful leads, and motivated to continue solely by the dubious interest I appeared to be eliciting, did I have anything better to do at the moment? My choice fell, for the conveniences it offered, on the following excerpt, one fairly significant to the story,* as it happens.

The narrator placed an ad one day in his local paper, expressing a desire to part with a family heirloom. This consisted of an altar vase in Jerusalem glass (described as faithfully as is possible within

....

* The reader will forgive me for not reproducing the manuscript's exact wording, it no longer being in my possession—as he will learn in the course of his reading. Let him credit me, nonetheless, over and above the dryness inherent in all summaries, with an effort toward complete fidelity.

the space of a classified ad) whose companion piece had been lost several years earlier (hence, on the narrator's part, and despite the grace of this object which would from then on be a single, unpaired item, the obtrusive feeling of an irreconcilable imbalance and the intention to deliver himself from it).

The anonymous ad ended with the classic formula: "If interested, write to box such-and-such, care of the paper." But, by an odd happenstance, the only response to his offer came from the narrator's own lady friend (the famous *Belle Dame*). She, not having been notified in advance, had thought this the long-lost double and had planned to surprise her partner with it. The misunderstanding would have been no more than amusing were it not for the troubling conclusion Desiderio provided: It seemed, subsequently, that this mismatched vase of vertiginous effect had regained a strange kind of integrity and had become—these were the narrator's own words: *order itself.*

It goes without saying that at this point I had no lady friend, no altar vase, nor even any family heirloom, and my own vertiginous effects came from a different source. But it mattered little, insofar as the first act of the drama—the classified ad in some run-of-the-mill V. gazette—fell within the scope of my competence. And *I didn't expect to go any further.* So convinced was I of the deed's futility (it being well understood that this was a caprice, the mere setting down of a landmark amid the uniform days: the ad day like the museum day . . . without which, would there have been any *time*?) that I even planned to alter the text. I recall, in particular, that I dearly regretted having destroyed the lithograph of **** which was every bit as good as Jerusalem glass—and perhaps I might have sold it! for I of all people should know that one doesn't follow an author to the letter.

JEAN LAHOUGUE

But I had no lithograph anymore. I was in no mood, for all that, to draft an ad of pure fantasy. And so it was by default and through laziness that I repeated, for the benefit of readers of chain verse, Desiderio's exact terms, regarding it as a whim priced at ten francs a line.

Improbably, two days later, I received a laconic reply through the gazette. Someone claimed to be *intéressé* (this masculine adjective depriving me, however, of all hope that I might see some sort of *Belle Dame* come out of the woodwork) in my offer. He invited me to get in touch with ?, a name that meant nothing to me—badly written, moreover, and barely legible—whose address followed, I recall, and was in V., on rue des Douves Anciennes, i.e., Old Moats Street.

At this point in my account, the reader will perhaps be able to conceive of the vague distress that began to settle over me—vague because I could see no tragic event that would provide the key. On the contrary: it derived instead from the fact that things were going too well, were within a few turns of coming too close to my most intuitive visions (which sprang from an adolescent, romantic imagination), to my desires. It would be as if you were hungry for an orange and one was right there, in the first sideboard you opened.

Of course, the natural reaction to the dim manifestation of such a power is, first of all, a feeling of supreme confidence. (And I thought pityingly of Sergeant L., the inspector's dogsbody, who was spending his Sundays laboriously piecing together Desiderio's torn-up story.) But anxiety quickly takes hold when one thinks: "What if, rather than dreaming of extraordinary but happy adventures because such is the law of the genre, I were to slip up and imagine that my life, say, was in jeopardy?" Thus, when too many desires are realized, desire itself is to be feared.

It is to be conjectured that I never engaged in such speculations explicitly. I simply felt some of their repercussions. Among others: The more I told myself that there were no grounds for auguring unpleasant outcomes to this story, that such things mustn't even be thought of, the more my imagination set to work envisioning them, and what had been my exaltation fled.

More immediately, to the aforementioned distress was added this simple realization: I had a dizzying absence of anything to offer. I'd proposed only words—and second-hand words at that, since they'd been dictated by Desiderio. My first impulse, therefore, was to write to my art lover on rue des Douves Anciennes and tell him he was too late. Everything would have then been said.

Next, in response to these same anxieties, I had the childish certainty that this was a coward's trick. (And, come to think of it: hadn't the example set by the young Araucanian boy who paused at the threshold of a legendary palace, brushing the door mechanism with his fingertips a ritual number of times without knowing it, and whose courage consisted only of refusing the absurdity of having come this far for nothing: he stepped inside, become *natural* to me?) It seemed to me I'd sunk in someone's (?) estimation, someone I imagined behind me as in times past, with delight.

I didn't send the note. On the contrary. I took a stroll through the neighborhood of rue des Douves Anciennes with the idea that simply seeing the house would be enough (and I thought: *seeing a house justifies everything, essentially*). I walked past it twice, a villa outside the town walls, fronting on the lane that crossed the moat, near the main gate. I stole a glance at the mailbox, where there was no name. I would have waited and watched for someone's arrival had there been a hiding place—but there was none. I walked back up the lane so as not to arouse suspicion. I even chewed a sprig of bittersweet, to further underline my indifference. Hadn't I done all that was needed to consider myself square with my obligations? but—this is just it—what obligations?

That very evening, haunted by who-knows-what remorse, I decided to go back. I'd waited for my landlady to leave before undertaking a methodical search of number 11, which was a trove of old-fashioned junk of every description. And I finally found what I was looking for under some flowers: an altar vase that, though it didn't tally exactly with Desiderio's description, wasn't so far off as to prevent it passing. I calculated that, should it interest my correspondent, I could always tell Madame Vian I'd accidentally broken it, even at the risk of paying her ten times its actual value.

(I remember this ridiculous evening on which I hesitated once again to set foot outside, because apparently there was to be no end to my wandering the streets of V. laden with preposterous objects, when vacations were a time for going empty-handed! The vase, even wrapped in newspaper, seemed to me every bit as humiliating as a bridegroom's bouquet. Thank goodness it was nighttime.)

The streets were unusually deserted for such a warm evening. My shoes creaked, being new, or nearly new. My package kept slipping from my hands, possibly because I bore no love for the thing, and I was compelled to adopt all sorts of disagreeable holds. I was on the point of turning back when I had the ludicrous feeling that the noise of my shoes and the newsprint, *superadded* to the sounds of my first passage, would cause—and rightly so—a scandal. To continue on my way seemed less sonorous.

Many of the facades were lit—because they deserved to be—but only just, as this was neither July nor August. These illuminations reflected what seemed to me an entirely unfair hierarchy, given that many admirable architectural specimens had been forgotten, and no longer officially existed—I was relying on memory and would have liked to confirm their presence by touch, were it not for my burden—the principal church itself being no more than its parvis, the illuminated statues full of insects.

I can still recall two things in particular: the theater where a rehearsal could be heard, also only just, over my shoes and vase. Then, at the end of an endless street, a facade seemingly much more luminous than the rest, which was merely, beneath a simple neon lamppost, a blank wall.

I was hoping, I think, that the lights would have been extinguished in the villa on rue des Douves Anciennes (and perhaps I'd only come so late, despite the vase which was all too visibly my conscience, for this very reason). But they hadn't gone to bed. I could even hear a voice, bizarrely calm and anachronistic (I later learned it was Marlene Dietrich in *My Blue Heaven*), which, in the dark, and therefore in the absence of modern objects like a low-slung car or a TV aerial, etc. to immediately refute it, intensified my uneasiness.

A man in a smoking jacket opened the door to me, a man whom I had difficulty recognizing as the inspector because he was standing silhouetted against the light.

JEAN LAHOUGUE

It was like a burlesque comedy. Morand as master of ceremonies—at the very moment I was counting on scoring a decisive point against him, on widening, as they say, my *lead*—while *My Blue Heaven* and vague whisperings could be heard, and me with the altar vase in newspaper. Morand seemed surprised, but only just.

"I should've known it was you . . ."

He hesitated for a beat, then:

"On the other hand, I couldn't have predicted you'd turn up tonight."

And to explain these words, in the background, the clinking of glasses, *My Blue Heaven*:

"I'm entertaining a few friends. You're welcome to join us."

I made no move to duck out of it, conscious of having committed what error? and impelled by what stupid hope of redeeming it? while in the very uniform of submission (the sweater jacket I'd been wearing since my arrival in V., my scarf, my vacation clothes—dusty from their trip through the attic of number 11).

Soon I was stepping into a sumptuous, somber, and tasteful living room, amid his *habillé* friends (smoking jackets like Morand's for the men; long, metallic dresses with plunging V-necks for the women, in comparison with which—forgetting what I'd been, down to the smallest niceties of decorum—I felt I was gauche and naked and my shoes too new), with glass in hand, as if at the halfway point, neither to toast nor to drink.

I never left Morand's side. He knew, and that was reassuring. Whereas the others, I thought, would never understand the reasons for my comical presence here, the explaining of which—assuming they even wanted to hear it—would have forced me to go far back into the past, all the way to Paris, it was impossible, so that to me they would be definitively pre-Paris strangers, and thus doubly alien: besides, they were smiling. Because of them, I brushed at my clothes from time to time, by guesswork, as if they were completely coated in dust. My eyes never left Morand, and I gave the impression of being quite fond of him.

I was surprised that the first thing he spoke to me about was *My Blue Heaven* (then about his prewar records, for Morand was a collector of voices. He told me as much, and this was, more than an expression of vanity, a means of frustrating my Desiderio curiosity. But this flaw made him seem more brotherly to me . . . He showed me the phonograph with its stylus and horn, which I touched). Only then, in dribs and drabs, between asides to one stranger or another in the living room, which I didn't understand and which were blanks, he told me that his department was, in fact, going through the classifieds . . .

"Yours reminded me of something—you know very well what: the sergeant is a diligent worker."

"You were waiting, it seems to me, for the sea to deliver you a body?"

"Which doesn't mean I can't be surprised by certain coincidences. Reading, twenty-four hours apart, the same text from two ostensibly different authors, does that seem *normal* to you?"

"Why bother with the complication of a letter, when you could have just sent a man around to the newspaper office?"

"The Morelle case, until we have proof to the contrary, doesn't exist."

He added:

"I've answered your questions. Will you answer mine? Where did you get the text of your ad?"

I confessed. He made me no reproach.

"My wife," he said.

She walked past.

The inspector's other remarks—the remains—were of no account. Nor were mine, I hope. Aside from the fact that, one after the other, we placed our hands on the slender horn (I have no recollection, from the moment I disencumbered myself of the vase on a round table in the foyer, of ever having had my hands anywhere else that evening).

I caught a glimpse, while Morand was speaking to yet another unknown woman behind her back, at the far end of the living room, in the shadow of a staircase, of two child-sized figures in pale pajamas who'd sneaked out of their beds just to *see* us. It seemed to me, either despite or because of this, that nothing more could possibly happen.

But then a merry person said to me, handing me a drink from behind the table, that as they were fresh out of utopias today, they'd sell me this glass. And it's here that I'll take up my subject again, because the person in question was Vanessa.

It must be admitted that the way I approached this woman was far from glorious. For that matter, I'd begun to feel a certain lack of self-assurance in everything I did, to the point that I sometimes wondered, thinking of Paris: How had I ever managed not to be shy? and I wouldn't have a clue.

Long after the party on rue des Douves Anciennes, it would occasionally happen that I'd break a vase when trying to change the water. Or, then again: the imperfection of one of Vanessa's records (the dull roar suggestive of an ocean close behind) would so nettle me that I'd give her the exact same record, but new, two or three times over. Certain scratches humiliated me.

From the first days of our relationship (I'm not even speaking anymore of the party, where I was so ill-dressed that I had every excuse in the world for being tongue-tied. I'm thinking rather of our lunch at the Palazzo two days later, when I should, at the very least, have shown a little confidence) I experienced a strange difficulty in saying what needed to be said and in getting a proper grip on things. As if the memory of that vase slipping from my hands, on the night we jokingly called that of our engagement, had become the rule of my life.

I recall the big dining room of the Palazzo (a fancy hotel in V.) with its line of obsequious servers who let no desire of ours escape them, and its high theatrical arrases. There was a frightful repeating border pattern around the tops of the walls and on the lampshades at the tables (such that all private intimacy seemed necessarily echoed to the rafters), of the type known, I believe, as a *Vitruvian scroll*, waves unrolling indefinitely one after the next, with neither beach nor end: I can still see them in my mind's eye. Finally, mirrors covered the walls—and even the door at the far end of the room, directly opposite me, so that my image was flung aside (at the

JEAN LAHOUGUE

moment when, out of shyness, I was watching myself in it) whenever someone entered.

And I told Vanessa, in all innocence, that she reminded me of another woman: the *Belle Dame* of the manuscript in my possession (the same way I might have sworn I'd seen her somewhere before), not even knowing whether this was tactless, ridiculous … A short time later, I would see nothing indelicate about fretting over her lovers.

But she showed, toward me, the same patience one shows toward adolescents. She defended herself against everything with a gentle touch. Her lovers had nothing to do with me (it was the line of obsequious servers who, in their mocking way, had very much to do with me, never letting me out of their sight). She had never known any Morelle. She could enjoy utopias and jolly evenings among friends without being, for all that, an "other woman"—and a silent waiter came over to refill our glasses.

Vanessa C., according to the portrait she sketched of herself that day at the Palazzo, was no very extraordinary young woman. She was from Paris. She belonged to the *École du Louvre* (as one might say one belonged to the Fontainebleau School, which confirmed exactly what for me?). She was interested in V. and was, at present, "involved in a work on its architecture." The utopias on Sunday had been a defense against the allurements of the past. She'd met the Morands one day through mutual friends. She'd been to rue des Douves Anciennes several times for the regular, *cheery* parties with which I was already acquainted. It was there she'd encountered, not too long ago, a timorous, nosy man who'd become an impossible lover, on the subject of whom I demanded more details (through Desiderian curiosity or some vague jealousy: could I have said which?), in my blindness, since the man was myself.

(That *impossible* qualifying *lover* merits a pause here. It will be understood that it contributed no more to my glory than the blunders and indelicacies already reported. And if I describe, with some embarrassment, the failure of my early sexual relations with Vanessa, it is less from a desire to abase myself than as a form of conjuration [or adjuration?], as it was, much later, to appear to me.

We'd gone to rue de Palaevouno, where she had her room. Strangers were loitering on the landing, and so we practically dashed inside. Could they hear or see us at all? I imagine that an awareness of the temptation our door presented to others stimulated us, though we didn't admit it to ourselves. What with this, my extended celibacy, and the sheer beauty of Vanessa's body, which I'd been undressing for so long, wall after wall, that it was naked too late, perhaps?, I *missed* this body, in such a humiliating manner that the obscene image of my failure is forever graven on my memory. And so, the semen which rushed out too quickly and spread over Vanessa's white thigh forms a blot, henceforth, on every white page I see.

That night at Morand's when I'd felt so ill at ease, when the only *esprit* I'd shown was, as they say, *de l'escalier*—where the children were—may have cast a pall of consternation over the nights to come. Perhaps Vanessa's body was too perfect as well—I mean: without the sagging of buttocks and breasts, or the areolas as big and dark as inkblots, that fill me with tenderness, and which I need in order to introduce therein my pleasure or my sanction.

Of course, later on our relations *normalized*. But on that night, the first night, I proved incapable of renewing the slightest contact, and more than this: I invented and shammed some sort of head pain to account for my inadequacy. And even now, aren't I still trying to explain away the difficulties and heartbreak that lay in store for us by means of this one night's delay?)

From that moment on, I should have given no more thought to Desiderio. And, in fact, it seems to me I wasn't far from just this state of forgetting. When Madame Vian stopped by on rue de Nazareth of an evening, instead of pressing her with questions about Morelle (questions she invariably turned to her own purposes by using them to talk about things from an earlier era) I'd say yes, and no, and nothing more, so that her stories—always the same—sank into the sands, and she left all the sooner.

In the beginning, it wasn't because I was losing interest in the case: I was simply eager to get back to Vanessa, and Madame Vian's chitchat would have greatly postponed our reunion. But eventually, by ceasing to ask questions, I was very near ceasing to care. Only the despondency I gradually discerned in my landlady, which grieved me, would induce me to ask her a *peripheral* question, for example:

"Did Morelle seem happy?"

which would make her stay a while longer and give her pleasure (there was pleasure for me, too, I realized, in piquing my own impatience and whetting my desire). And all the while, I was ignorantly nurturing such a baneful curiosity, essentially from sentimentality!

After the grandmother's departure, it became my habit to slip out the back and head to rue de Palaevouno. I was sneaking, or nearly sneaking, and on arrival I would sneak again, owing to the people I risked drawing out onto the landing. We met on rue de Palaevouno rather than at my place, probably because Vanessa took the idea of being talked about, as they say, less to heart—but had I ever actually asked her?

We'd eat something light and make love, I seeking on her, already, something to discomfit her, because it was necessary—it seemed to me—, because I would thereby gain knowledge, because there would be, yet again, something to conjure away by means of possession, such as minuscule flaws, a bit of what they call orange-peel skin . . .

The room, which was Vanessa's ordinary setting, contributed to this degradation—and this would be another reason in support of my preference for rue de Palaevouno, a preference that no longer owed anything to the fear of scandal, quite the contrary—through its many touches of squalor: the remains of our meal, for example, or the washing area, not concealed by any curtain nor tucked away in the wings, where she'd perform her ablutions, the upturned bag in a corner, and the door I could see from the bed.

(I recall that this door, full of gilt decorations, gave directly onto the landing. It was never locked—but I don't know whether this was through my own negligence or Vanessa's, and was it really negligence? The fact remains that it could have been opened by a third party at any time, mistakenly or otherwise. And so its porcelain knob—what I chose to call porcelain, obviously—that gleamed, that I clasped inwardly, and the peeling gilt flakes that trembled, were, as much as Vanessa's sex, perhaps, the locus of my pleasure.)

Afterward, I'd have a cigarette. I'd open the window because of the smoke. And it seemed to me that it was this open window—God-knows-what power of effacement—that entitled me to ask my questions in spite of everything (the very ones, or within a hair's

JEAN LAHOUGUE

breadth, that I was no longer asking my landlady except in cases of emergency), to suggest to Vanessa an idiosyncrasy, a habit of such-and-such a lover—whom she'd acknowledged the day before to put an end to my inquisition—in order to make his image coincide with Desiderio's, I believed. To which she'd reply, not without justice, that the truth was I wished her to have had no lovers except those in my own image.

This was how, on the day when I should have stopped thinking about Desiderio, when I'd been circulating in V. for so long that it had ceased to amaze me, when I could have departed, therefore, without a pang (the way certain old folks, already blind and deaf, don't really die but *pass*), I was detained there.

Vanessa had to finish her internship in the town and I had to return to Paris because my vacation was nearing its end. I remember wandering the streets of V., not knowing what my resolution should be, so lost in thought that I sometimes wound up talking to myself—about the gleaming porcelain knob, about squalor and gold—: there was always some onlooker present to observe me.

(Among others, I remember an old woman. She was giving me such disapproving looks that my childish reaction was to put on a show of complete lunacy for her benefit, and so I gravely took out a paper that was in my pocket—still the same one, but filthy now and covered in bits of loose tobacco—, crumpled it slowly as I stared the old woman down, then dropped it, making it into a sort of ball, or rather a lagger, which with a one-legged hop I sent hurtling straight at her hell-square. She scurried off.)

At times, I told myself Vanessa C. was a vacation within my vacation, life itself, and regarding my professional obligations I had that rebellious feeling one sometimes gets when *well fixed*: with as little as two or three months' cash on hand—two or three months' lead?—: this lagging behind, however, on the essential, who imposes that on me, and on what grounds? Also: following in my wake, among the tourists with guidebook in hand, who existed in such numbers as to divert me, was one individual, I imagine, who would have been only too glad to see the back of me.

At other times, I nevertheless had half a mind to catch the next train. Specifically, I recall an unpleasant scene near the fountain square where something was missing (I knew it to be the shouts of swarms of children) because the children were all standing, nearly stock still, around a dog belonging to one of them that had been run over, and some shards of glass. The car must have kept on going: there were none to be seen. The child wanted to pet the corpse, whose muzzle was oozing blood—he was held back, and someone came with a wheelbarrow, which was as much as to say: nothing more to be done here. Well, I thought, that was true enough.

Further. Must it be said that these two images contrasted? I mean: the dead dog and Vanessa C., the bleeding maw and the sex. Contrasted, or blended into one another, the one becoming the other's shame, or its renunciation, or its atonement, or its remorse? That I was going around in circles while mulling this over in V. was proof that I could no longer see my way out.

When I looked up, I found myself in front of the main post office, a long, classical-style building with a stair so prodigiously made that ascending it to drop a letter in the box was a mere trifle. I wrote a note to ***, coeditor of the press, with whom I maintained friendly relations. In it, I pleaded an urgent, unforeseen hold-up—I spoke of a moral crisis of some kind. I deliberately omitted my address, as much to protect myself from guilt trips appealing to my sense of duty as to provide corroborating evidence for the turmoil I was in—according to me.

VII

Time had passed, and I thought I knew all the streets quite well, when I discovered what I jokingly called the town's cunt. What I mean is: one of those hidden places that exist in every city, and that who-knows-what revulsion condemns to perpetual shame: somehow no one ever really stops there. This was a detached house in a sort of Composite style, abandoned—in consequence doubly refuse in V., where architectural unity was scrupulously maintained—on a scrap of manor grounds that must have been subdivided into lots very early on, and which no longer existed: a folly.

I made this discovery by chance on my umpteenth trip around the city, one of those that had scarcely any purpose now beyond passing the time until evening, motivated more by Vanessa's absence—she worked during the day—than by any pursuit of Desiderio, in whom I no longer believed save through force of habit. Even so, it was to a conjunction of fairly ridiculous circumstances that I owed my attention being drawn to it.

Since the street avoided both beaten paths and official beauties, it was unfrequented. I therefore had ample opportunity to observe the doings of the young man I was preceding by a short distance, and who, whenever I turned my head, assumed the now-familiar attitude of an art lover studying the houses. But when we reached the aforementioned folly (it clashed and grated on the nerves in such a way that no one gave it a glance), his crude alibi fell apart, and my young man lost his composure. I was sure I'd unmasked him. I carried on, however, as if nothing had happened, but followed such a lunatic course that his tailing me soon became blatant.

We'd doubled back, retracing our steps past the bishops' residence that houses the Utopias Museum, when at the entrance to the chapter house I literally assaulted my pursuer. He looked at me in terror and struggled ineffectually to free himself from my grasp, all while spluttering imprecations.

He was a very young man indeed, and I had some difficulty picturing him as one of Morand's duty officers. He was every inch the innocent student on a trip, the boy from a good family who was stunned by my challenging him. I demanded he explain himself nonetheless, cornering him with a few incontrovertible facts (or which seemed incontrovertible to me—one could not, at any rate, set down to pure chance the clear-cut repetition of certain actions and facial expressions). But there was in his protestations such apparent good faith, such tones of sincerity when he swore he had no idea what I was talking about, that little by little I relaxed my grip.

I remember there were people walking around us. At no point were they tempted to intervene, probably so used to these exchanges of words that the sight had become familiar: they smiled to themselves. I found myself so disarmed that my attitude slowly changed, and I came round at last to making my apologies to the young man. I even said, with an inconsistency he was kind enough to overlook (in truth, I was not so convinced by his denials that I felt I had to abandon my interrogation—but I understood the need to do it in a more civilized fashion), that I'd made a mistake. In brief, I acquitted myself so well that he agreed to have a drink with me to show there were no hard feelings.

It was as we came within sight of a bar (called, inanely, "du Commerce," and none other than that in which I had stopped on my first day) that I had the sudden feeling something was amiss.

The explanation was quite simple: what I had before me was the companion piece of the detached house with the dilapidated entrance. But this one, occupied by the café, was unobjectionable—that is to say: rectified, replastered, whitewashed. It was separated from its twin by a full block of more recent houses. Such that the other one, fresh in my mind, was either this one's shriveled origin or its final disgrace, as if not existing in the present, not possible, hence the vertiginous feeling and the idea, perhaps—to explain both my stubborn desire to return to the vicinity and the fears that, a hundred times over, had kept me away—of *labia minora*.

We entered the bar, my companion and I, and seated ourselves at the counter. There must have been a billiard table in the back room, because we heard the sound of balls (like tired footfalls on a staircase, but then there would suddenly come a few shots in such quick succession that it was like someone stumbling, so it seemed, and these were so violent that I jumped every time). Two customers in black wearing neckties were discussing inheritance. Someone said: "What'll it be?"

The funny thing is, I'd brought the young man there to get him to talk. Yet I myself was at a loss for words. No longer able to ask him point-blank why he was so interested in me, I groped in vain for a roundabout way of drawing at least some small clue out of him. As if, after getting physical, we'd both become filled with timidity, we remained silent for a long while.

There intervened at this point a circumstance out of the ordinary, connected—it's true—with the awkwardness we felt during our silence, from which it was necessary to distract ourselves by some trifling activity (others would have put on a record or begun to whistle): I'd spilled a little milk on the counter and was, with the end of my teaspoon, as one does absently when on the phone, endowing the blob with arms and legs—a semblance of meaning. Then I saw that the young man was doing the very same at the bottom of his empty glass, to a blotch that was, in his case, imaginary. But this concordance, which was in no way premeditated, and which we noticed simultaneously, was enough to make us laugh. And then talk.

I told him what I thought about V., since he was interested in towns, and this, in particular, because I was still marveling over it: that even if one knows a neighborhood like the back of one's hand, one still has everything to learn about it—case in point, these two houses. And I tacked on a sort of moral at the end, to the effect that one can never be sure of anything until the second time around, that one never discovers but always rediscovers, and other such platitudes.

At first he replied in the same confiding manner. We traded old memories. I'd almost forgotten my mistrust—a few minutes longer and I would have been even more direct and frank (with that certainty one feels among friends that one can always be more so). When, with a chance word, a turn of phrase, my suspicions were revived.

Please understand: this feeling was nothing extraordinary, or, at least, if there was an extraordinary quality, it was only its violence. Whether this was because my companion had joined me too eagerly in the confiding manner mentioned above, or because we'd quite literally traded memories, by which I mean: to the point that we no longer knew which belonged to whom, I had the impression that the young man was reciting a lesson expressly designed to please me.

For example, he said: "Just seeing a town is enough to make me happy," or "I love V., which is close to the ocean," "V. is under threat: the authorities should protect it," "There are no truly normal streets," "I always walk on the shady side, what about you?," "Do you know Florence?," etc. (all phrases I've retained because they responded, let us say: to temptations, but he said them *as asides*, the way one might drop a quotation).

No doubt my first reaction was to blame Morand, whose henchman this boy, against all appearances, might well have been (I vowed to put this question to the inspector). If not, and this worry, which might appear absurd, became more and more acute as he professed feelings so strangely patterned on my own, while I bit back my confidences, my sympathy: How had I ever been able to feel the least brotherly feeling toward someone without seeing it as a trap?

Back on rue de Nazareth, still preoccupied with this last thought (though it was personal, and could have waited), I reproached myself for having given the young man only half an ear toward the end (I even asked myself questions such as: Had I paid? How had we parted? On good terms? etc.). Madame Vian was there and number 11 was a true resting place, an altar of repose.

She'd seen me in town with the other man. She asked me in passing if I'd made some friends. To which I replied no, he was a Parisian (as I would have said "a tourist") looking for the bishops' residence, and I'd accompanied him, having a few notions about architecture and history. She picked up on the mention of Paris in this little white lie (which I'd told so as not to worry her) because Paris was where her son had lived before the war. He'd had, she told me, a brilliant career ahead of him there.

She was changing the water in the vases as she talked about her child, and it was then that, in an effort to help her, I broke the one that distantly resembled Desiderio's description, and on the subject of which I could lay claim to my own share of memories. Perhaps on this account, it seemed to me she ought to feel more vexation over its loss than she would have for any other. But, to my great surprise, she was rather pleased. She had enough vases to replace it ten times over, and this was, apparently, a happy accident.

I wasn't much interested in what she said after that (I even recall, as a ridiculously precise detail, that I was taking great care not to cut myself on the pieces as I picked them up—my gestures were minute) until a word caught my attention.

It had to do with a house, yet again, at the very moment I was turning over in my mind, like some bizarre object, this bit of reasoning, whether originating in the young man or myself I could no longer tell: Was there ever anything besides houses? and, more specifically, with one this son had supposedly bought in V. after making his fortune, and which he'd never gotten the chance to enjoy.

She spoke of this purposeless house in bitter terms. ***, the son, had scarcely installed the basic furnishings before he'd died. She assured me she hadn't been able to pass it since without pain. I imagined, for this reason, that perhaps it might be the derelict house. The truth is that I was still trying to reduce the unknown to the known, and from these two mysteries make one straightforward fact. I could then tell myself that a loose end had been tied up and move on to something else. Was it because I seemed so relieved that Madame Vian had to specify, as if to lend more substance to her son's house through a naive detail that enhanced its value: "There's a garden out back"?

That same week, I returned once again to see Morand. I'd arrived at the conclusion that the surveillance of which I was the object would serve as my pretext. This in itself proved that other people were interested in the case. And, apart from this interest taken by others—it being understood that I, for my part, now had reasons for staying in V. unrelated to Desiderio—had there been any developments in the case? and was there still a case at all?

The reason I hadn't come to this decision sooner was that I'd thought it was Morand doing the surveillance. I was afraid he'd confirm it for me. I was willing to submit tamely to being followed, so long as it was possible—and exhilarating—for me to believe that it wasn't just the inspector who was taking an interest in my words and deeds.

Now I was tired. The confirmation that had hitherto been so dreaded would, I thought, free me from Desiderio. Once I'd moved past Desiderio, it seemed to me, with extravagant naivete, then my happiness with Vanessa C. would be even more profound—or better still (liberated from all those pernicious questions I was heaping upon Vanessa in spite of myself, from that obsession I had with seeking *another woman* behind her every minor gesture): *indisputable*. It mattered little to me that, in doing so, I'd be admitting that Morand had been right and joining him in his detached indifference.

But the answer he gave was not what I'd been expecting. He vehemently denied having ordered the surveillance. He seemed to me, on this occasion, more preoccupied, more irritable than he'd been the other times. I felt ridiculous because he wasn't a person to whom one came to lay down arms. He didn't abandon his sarcastic tone, but, curiously enough, it didn't faze me.

"In a town like V.," he told me, "everybody watches everybody. The locals the tourists because they're a diversion. The tourists the locals because they're the past, the living component of the historical monuments, of the *art*. When I was first assigned here, I thought it was the civilians watching the police, there were so many eyes on me, and me the disorder!"

"With the result that," I said, "after a life divided between informing on others and inventing stories (not to mention doing Sunday puzzles) the people here disappear without a trace, all for the authorities' greater comfort and convenience . . ."

"No one but you gives a damn about Morelle. No one but you has even tried to find evidence he existed. And you lied to me! Well? Who's paying you? The feds? God the Father? and why? so you can judge some crazy old woman's level of dementia in my place? What would you expect me to open an investigation on if not *your* comings and goings?"

"No one sent me. I've given up any intention (if I ever had one) of intruding on your bailiwick—and, in a way, that's the main thing I've come here to tell you."

"Are you saying you've decided to leave us?"

"I'm staying on in V. for other reasons."

All of a sudden, it seemed to me that something out of the ordinary was happening, as if everything were set for a showdown of which I knew neither the causes nor the stakes (I remember we both involuntarily looked down, with a synchronicity that was probably comical, at the ammonite, and the bizarre, idiotic thought occurred to me that we were doing so in order to *try* our gazes), but he asked me, almost gently:

"Your other reasons go by the name of Vanessa C., right?"

"I see you're admirably well-informed. It's true, everybody does watch everybody in V."

"And you claim to have lost interest in Morelle?"

This time, I started.

"What's the connection between him and Vanessa? What are you hiding from me? The first time, you implied that Morelle was a myth. A minute ago you were acting as if you thought I'd dreamed him up myself. Now you're linking the name of this alleged phantasm to the only thing here that's real to me, or ever will be, whether you care to believe it or not. Why? Why are you trying to sweep this story under the rug?"

At this point, I must admit, to my shame, that I'd crossed the line, and that my very excessiveness was preventing Morand—even supposing he felt inclined to unburden himself—from taking me into his confidence. As I might have expected, after giving me a long stare, he checked the time on his wrist with that expression of stupid surprise he'd used on me before to convey that it was inconceivably late. I didn't insist.

At the door, he told me (in the same formulaic terms as the first time—back then it was to invite me to live a little!—with the result that, one piece of advice canceling out the other, it was as if I'd never visited this drab gray police station):

"If I were you, I wouldn't see Mademoiselle C. again. I'd go back to my responsibilities in Paris. I'd stick to my books from here on out..."

I found myself out in the hall, dumbfounded. There were young officers who all looked alike, in doorways that all looked alike. The sound of a typewriter could be heard, being operated by someone who barely knew how: there was no end of silences. One felt, in one's fingertips, the intention to fill them as a way of coming to the rescue (of whom? I pictured Sergeant L. plugging away in a dismal office with a calendar featuring illustrations of the seasons: a woodland scene for autumn, Mont Blanc for winter, a flowering garden for spring, a woman for summer—on the wall). But since everything was extremely slow compared to the images, dreads, and suspicions running through my mind, it was I—so I thought—who was moving too fast, as in that disorder known as mentism, I believe.

Out on the street (so Morand's eye wasn't following me—eyes, I should say: would they be comical from now on, the gentleman in the glasses, the fat lady, the respectable young man, or malevolent? Their faces were a contrasting, ill-assorted lot in my memory), I had an even harder time collecting my thoughts. I believed there were footsteps behind me: my temples.

I recall that, in the midst of this confusion, it would happen that I'd stop dead in my tracks, flooded by a single, overriding emotion: pain, for example, and I'd notice I was at the exact place the dog had been run over, in the fountain square. Or rage: I'd be walking past the bishops' residence. I'd turn around to look, and there would be nothing.

A few shopkeepers and old men were out smoking on their doorsteps. I detoured around them. I'd probably imagined myself returning home free, meaning: without any Desiderio curiosity, therefore without the feeling that the people who confronted me were leading me down the garden path—their silence ceasing to be a deliberate omission, becoming, in short, *natural* once again (in which case I would have gladly bought wine, or fruit, for the meals with Vanessa C. on rue de Palaevouno, in the absence of showier offerings). Instead of which, with my curiosity rekindled, these same silences gave me proof of unknown hatreds.

(Among others, I drifted, without meaning to, toward the road overlooking the railway junction over which I'd laid my hand. I remember there wasn't a breath of wind, so that the puffs of smoke rose scarcely higher than they would have inside a house.) But it's only today that I wonder, somewhat foolishly, whether or not I wanted to flee.

Such a state of mind, which the reader will have to pardon, should he detest as much as I do the showy display of discontent in books, as being drama of the cheapest variety, had an effect on my relationship with Vanessa.

The very evening of my conversation with Morand and my detours to avoid the doorstep smokers, something had changed. I still had questions to ask, but I'd lost the ability to make them impertinent (when I wanted to, when, the theatrical and slightly sadistic pleasure of my inquisition palling, I would seek out other tortures) by shifting the Desiderio mystery onto Morand—which I had considered easy. That evening, they'd become so imperative that I didn't put them into words but, possessing myself of Vanessa with the idea that she might be a physical threat to me, or perhaps only an obstacle to my search for the truth, but in either case on the *opposing side*, it was clear that I was investing my pleasure itself with their full cruelty.

In spite of, or maybe because of, which, the nights that followed were probably the most strangely happy of our time together (strangely, because I was wondering: Who is she? What does she want? What do her orgasms mean—or conceal? and in all this, Desiderio? but I held back my demand for as long as I could before it overwhelmed me. Is it absurd, today, laughable, to believe that the answer's urgency was spent in the ejaculation, as its very principle, its validation, along with all desire?).

The nights, I say, and round about them: because, without realizing it, I was keeping a closer watch on Vanessa's gestures and, from wondering too often (for example when she peeled a piece of fruit in a spiral, or—I was about to say: on the contrary!—bandaged my hand [which, one night, in pulling off my own clothes, I'd cut deeply on a shard of vase that had mysteriously gotten caught in a fold] outstretched and opened upward to receive what?): What does she know?, it was impossible that the smallest of her movements wouldn't give some hint, constitute a proof, but again: of what?, her body took on a marvelous importance.

During this time, too, I showered her with gifts that at any other time I would have found perfectly silly—I'm thinking of the records I replaced one by one, the poppies and amaryllises abstracted from several of my landlady's bouquets to form one of my own unnoticed. Did I know, exactly, that such *attentiveness* (which, to all appearances, she found touching) was for me actually vigilance, or, if you prefer: something like an unconscious experiment, with the view of provoking God-knows-what extraordinary situation in which she might betray some sort of culpability? But she smiled, and I wonder: Did I feel any happiness on that account?

Yet these situations may indeed have been extraordinary after all. (Regarding the flowers, we looked up, for fun, in an old dictionary she had [a 1923 *Larousse* in two volumes] the exact name of some mysterious species I'd unknowingly introduced. And we were bounced from one article to another [as, when a child, wanting to learn all there was to know about love through words, I went from pubis to vagina, to vulva, to lips, back to pubis, according to the innumerable circles of elusive meaning; and I slammed the volume shut with as loud a noise as possible to dispel my disappointment].

Regarding the records, of which she thenceforth owned duplicates, we preferred to put on the scratchy song, knowing there was a pure song in reserve.

Regarding my injury, I remember Vanessa unrolling later, like a filthy kakemono, the elastic bandage bearing the imprint of my blackened blood and lymph, making as if she were going to conserve it, and me forbidding the act with so much abrupt violence that we both had to laugh.)

But should any conclusions have followed from this?

In those days, I was still spending part of the night at rue de Palaevouno. I'd leave between three and four in the morning, after a preliminary sleep. This presented no problem for me, because at that hour I was regularly awakened by various noises, which at first I believed to be coming from the building or the street, but which I fairly quickly had to admit were projections of my own brain. I'll say a word about them here to show how I was unwittingly registering and recording even incidental emotions. Their ambiguous afflux, at the end of my sleep, could legitimately pass for an external event.

The most frequent sound was that of a bottle being tossed onto the pavement—which was unlikely given the hour, and of which, moreover, I never found any evidence upon leaving. I imagine the incident of the vase, and in particular the fear of cutting myself on my own clothing, had made a stronger impression on me than it reasonably should have.

There was once, too, something like the tip of a pool cue striking my head (after I'd been hearing my blood pound against a bandage for a while, perhaps) and all sorts of sharp, melodramatic bangs issuing from windows, doors, books, or revolvers. I forget what else . . .

The most obvious result of such bursts of noise, real or imagined, was to abruptly dispel my drowsiness in favor of a lucidity that seemed all the more dizzying to me for being, in the absolute silence and blackness, deprived of all object.

Either for this reason, or because I had the idea that I hadn't exerted myself enough during the day to have any hope of falling back asleep, I felt the need, first, to touch Vanessa's body (but I didn't dare wake her, and my gesture remained inadequate), then to get a firmer grasp on other bodies. And if I'd formed the habit of rising, in short, between three and four in the morning, I believe it was primarily, though this may provoke a smile, so that I could brush against V.'s walls and mark my steps distinctly on her sidewalks.

As it happened, this arrangement suited Vanessa, who preferred to have her mornings to herself (I suppose it was disagreeable to her to start the day under the sign of a conjugality full of the fitful movements of awakening, bodily oils and secretions, etc.—the seamy side of her pleasure. Or, quite simply: she didn't want to wash up, to urinate, in front of me, as she would necessarily have to do since there was no curtain—sources of shame I would need to infer, in order to mold them, later, under circumstances I'll describe), as did I.

I'd return, then, to rue de Nazareth, making my shoes echo resoundingly—to ward off, I suppose, the memory of the Morand evening. After which I'd lie in my bed and mull over a number of ideas, of data? until early dawn.

Was I intentionally organizing (in the same spirit of exorcism?) the dream material that was to follow (calculating that, reinvested, such-and-such a coincidence that had struck me would cease to be unique, and therefore gratuitous, and therefore a problem)? The fact remains that after two or three waking hours, the images that haunted the balance of my sleep revolved around minor incidents that had aroused my vigilance. (Such as: I was in the streets of V., but it was day. On the doorsteps, at regular intervals, adults were standing and weeping with preposterous, hiccupping sobs. And I *knew* that the source of this pain was their dead dog [the worst pain—it was confided to me—because it was moreover ridiculous] but I could see no canine corpse, and everything was proceeding as if I, on my walk, were standing in for it. And other similar adventures.) But however nightmarish, these adventures comforted me because another loop, it seemed, had been closed, and I was free to go elsewhere.

In the end, perhaps I believed that nothing but Vanessa would remain—stripped bare, in some way, beyond her own nudity, of everything in this story that wasn't her: she herself would have to raise an objection to my illusion.

This happened one evening, and in regard to the house my landlady had mentioned, the one her son had—supposedly—bought before the war and never occupied.

I often relayed tidbits of Madame Vian's conversation to Vanessa. What could I have told her about V., which she knew as well as the shirt on her back? or about Desiderio, without galling her by too frequent comparisons to the fanciful idealization already known to the reader, without making her believe she was desired for no other reason than to suit the needs and accidents of a quest that negated her? Talking about rue de Nazareth was all I had left, whatever these little betrayals of my aged friend may have cost me.

It had seemed to me, on preceding evenings, that Vanessa had shown signs of impatience when I talked about the son, the night crossings he'd made over the river N., the network. I hadn't been on my guard, both because this was essentially ancient history and because I wasn't giving it the wholehearted telling that sometimes made it so stirring to me in the grandmother's rendition. I'd rambled on, since this ancient history was nevertheless the only new thing the day had brought me: we had to talk, love having been *made*.

But on this night Vanessa's irritation exceeded all bounds. I watched in alarm as she reacted with the most intense agitation to words that hardly deserved it (notwithstanding, I couldn't stop myself from pursuing my tale—which wasn't my tale and was therefore, in my eyes, in some absurd way, doubly innocent—out of cruelty? a need to know? it amounted to the same thing), going so far as to abuse me—accusing me, God knows why, of subjecting her to a continual interrogation, of preferring the rantings of a crazy woman to her—, slapping me with all her might, sobbing... I tried my best to calm her.

"Don't you understand," she said, "that everything that woman tells you is a lie from A to Z? That as far as the Resistance goes, her never-to-be-forgotten son died during the epuration? That your Mother Vian concocted a work of fiction for herself? and the house is a dream, too! her dream that that little piece of garbage would settle down in V., near her, throwing over Paris, career, *wife*... Do you understand that?!"

One can imagine how staggered I was by these far-fetched accusations, and even more so by the passion with which Vanessa had delivered them. How was this story any concern of hers? Why this manifest hatred for a poor old woman (whom—even had she been lying to me from day one—I freely pardoned) that no feminine jealousy justified? I recalled Morand's insinuations. I asked:

"Where did you hear all this?"

"I read it!" she replied.

And, seeing the pitiable way she looked at me, I asked myself if there was any word I could say to her that wouldn't be—voluntarily or involuntarily—a trap.

VIII

It would not be fair to say that from this day on our rapport deteriorated. I'd seem to be holding Vanessa responsible when, I'm now convinced, the misunderstanding originated with me, and further back. I had loved her, I thought, on the basis of an entirely literary coincidence (which was itself quite infantile: I recall that as a boy I loved Angelica in *Jerusalem Delivered*, and my love consisted, in fact, of delivering her—from what, precisely? herself?). Ever since the day at the Palazzo, I hadn't spoken to her at length, about Desiderio, about my landlady, about anything but what might be called, on a very symbolic level, my *family*. What young woman would not, through attrition of patience, have finally cast it back in my teeth, this family, with all those excesses of language of which one is capable in such situations! This, at least, was the simple explanation I found for her attitude, not ruling out the possibility that her attacks may have contained a grain of truth (likely drawn from the archival material on V. which, after all, she had to consult every day, the history of people intersecting with that of stones) of no importance.

(A thought comes to mind: I was inwardly calling her "Belladonna," but that wasn't her name. It was I who, for those silly literary reasons it would be useless to rehash, in attributing this equivocal name to her—"all parts of the belladonna plant [cf. the 1923 *Larousse* in two volumes], especially the berries, contain a potent poison, atropine, which dilates the pupils . . ."—was poisoning myself in poisoning her. Thus, I felt I was as culpable as she for the immoderate words she'd spoken.)

For this reason, even if she'd thereby corroborated Morand's innuendos, I saw her as less an enemy than a victim. Might I mention that this changed nothing in our relations? with the possible exception that, to my shame, I found in making love to her an ambiguous resurgence of pleasure, in which the need to mortify her competed with violence.

One day, when I hadn't awakened at the aforementioned hour and had departed from rue de Palaevouno much later, I noticed I'd left my watch behind at her place. I retraced my steps to the landing and there, though I knew exactly what I would find, opened the door with no warning whatsoever. In the far corner of the room, the only one lighted, Vanessa was urinating (in an outmoded faience bucket, the water closet—as they say in V.—being far away). Yet instead of begging her pardon, shutting the door, if not in front of, then at least behind me, inexplicably, I stared pointedly at Vanessa and, my hand on the porcelain knob, closed the door only with extreme slowness. She rose quickly, but nonetheless not immediately. She said nothing.

On other occasions, I managed to orient her body (fascinated by the risk—which was probably more vivid in my mind than in hers—obsessed as I was by the image of my pursuers—of a third party peeping through the crack, the keyhole, or turning the knob) spread open precisely in the axis of the doorway—did she understand this?

I remember, too, having rifled the bag that was always lying open on the table, overflowing with creams, ambergris, bits of cotton wool—less to spy on her than as a complement to possessing her, perhaps, out of perversity. Inside I found a miniature camera with a flashcube. It was at the end of the roll. I cocked it and, one night, used it to photograph Vanessa against her will in a deliciously obscene pose. This was the only occasion on which she rebelled (but later, whether there were other memories that mattered to her on the roll connected to this one—she didn't bother to expose it, though—or whether she attached less importance to it—yet she didn't do the task herself—she had me take the film to be developed and pick it up afterward).

Such were the most significant episodes in that thoughtless and tolerated tyranny, at the end of which, is it or is it not fair to say our rapport had deteriorated?

The most remarkable thing is that I made no change in my habits. They would lead me, I thought, to the truth, because nothing leads there half so well. The only difference was that my interest was no longer on the same things, but rather on the little alterations time made to them, if not in reality than at least in my perception (I mean that the same place, the square with the steps for example, was not the same as it had been yesterday, solely by virtue of the fact that today it was supplemented by yesterday's memory and was a bit more profound for it, a bit richer, weightier—the *boules* bumping down the steps having innumerable echoes).

And so I roamed the streets of V. in a state of intoxication that a casual observer might have likened to that of the early days. But, if there was intoxication, it was in the sense that a drunkard sees *more*, touches the walls to be sure of them, etc. This is scarcely an exaggeration, because it was during these same days that I saw everything in terms of strange series which, until then, had never struck me.

I'm speaking as much of the shopkeepers taking the air in their doorways, of the little clouds of cigarette smoke floating head-high every twenty or thirty paces, of the medallioned facades, each more beautiful than the last, one could almost say: in a game of one-upmanship, as of coincidences like the following, included for reference:

One day, when my eye was drawn to a group of some dozen skinned and cleaned hares in a shop window, a swarm of shouting children came through the square and I had the uneasy feeling of a vague correspondence. There were also those bevies of young women who watched me go by, and who, when I thought back on them, I recalled as being all alike, because I'd paid less attention to their faces than to the desire they'd aroused in me: this was the same.

Things got to such a point that I went, once, to the street where the folly-house stood—to demonstrate to myself, I believe, some kind of lucidity, the way one might look at one's finger while reckoning in the following way (absurd, of course, because this in and of itself attests to drunkenness): I see only one, therefore I'm not drunk!—in the hope of a singular monstrosity, and indeed it was one, with the moss on its tiered roofs, the leprosy of its ornaments and broken windowpanes. But instead of the expected lucidity, I asked myself: It is, this abandoned house, the sign of what absurd reckoning?

So haunted was I by the repetitions that there emerged in my mind an outlandish theory concerning my shadowers. For not only was I

JEAN LAHOUGUE

still, beyond all possible doubt, under surveillance, but this surveillance was taking forms at once more insidious and more invasive.

Someone would turn up at my door, or, even more dangerously, at Vanessa's, with a flimsy story at the ready designed to gain them entry: rag-and-bone men looking for cast-offs (at first I got rid of some old clothes, but presently, alarmed at their insistence, I slammed the door in their faces), self-proclaimed traveling salespeople, of the type who don't get straight down to business (the sale of God-knows-what life insurance policy or book-of-the-month-club subscription) but instead launch into sob stories: I never heard them out to the end, and would use my own foot to displace the one they'd thrust in the door.

One evening, spotting one of them on the landing at rue de Palaevouno, I told myself he might, after all, be some lover or admirer of Vanessa's, whom I'd believed to be dogging my heels only to the extent that all my roads led to her.

Then I passed in review all the forms he must, in that case, have fleetingly adopted before my eyes in V., a bizarre parade of phantoms to whom it was impossible to assign clear features: the young man from the Bar du Commerce (even the young man from the Bar du Commerce, so *normal* that his face escaped me), the old woman who'd watched me play hopscotch nearly on top of her, a certain server from the Palazzo, the gentleman who'd fondled the window, the lady at whom I'd conducted a one-sided conversation through the glass of a public phone booth, the guard at the Utopias, the man in his embrasure, the facade enthusiast! So ridiculous did it seem to envisage a like series of false bellies and other prostheses (all for—I added naively—the love of a woman!) that I quickly abandoned the supposition as ludicrous. In any case, I recalled having felt myself under surveillance well before meeting Vanessa.

As my thoughts turned to the question of exactly when it had started, the idea crossed my mind that the man from the square with the steps who'd returned my notes, or then again: the passersby who were curious about my nude, could well have already been it.

Going back even further, I thought of the traveler whose bag I'd nearly picked up on disembarking from the train. He was coming from Paris. Hence this hallucination, both dizzying and naive: my surveillance—I remembered such-and-such a drinking companion, people I'd jostled in crowds, all the strangers who cross your path and are all equally faceless, like spies—had it ever begun?

I smiled at this excess of imagination, brought on, in my opinion, by inactivity and confinement to the town (it was so captivating, V., and at the same time of a dullness so fittingly described as *deadly*, that in observing the doings of the curious man on the rue de Palaevouno landing, there flashed upon me a kind of detective novel I might have written, in the absence of living it, the long and the short of which would have been that certain settings can kill, as it's said certain cries can do, or certain forms of physical contact, in the long run. Thus it would be entitled, in obedience to the rules of the genre, *The Mystery of the Golden Door*, for example, this door being the author of the superlatively perfect crime . . .). Because of which—but was it a form of revenge?—I wished in spite of myself that such undesirables might be eyewitnesses to other excesses, able to give categorical testimony.

From my landlady's attitude, in particular, I understood that a change had taken place. I might perhaps have been showing some

　　　　　　　　　　　　　　　　　　　JEAN LAHOUGUE

reserve, without realizing it, since Vanessa had vilified her more than was necessary. But the intoxication I mentioned may, too, have been more apparent to her than to myself, and her silence on the matter a sign of sympathy. For it seemed to me that she had, little by little, been neglecting her confidences (giving me only, at first, by dribs and drabs, fragmentary information on the peacetime office her son had fixed up for himself—according to her own taste, the listener suspected—in the imaginary house, then falling silent— seeing that this was cutting no ice with me, no doubt), she now had only actions for and around me.

These were actions that had become familiar, but which, abruptly deprived of commentary (had it served to justify them, then?), seemed to me unreasonably eccentric. (I remember her going up and down the stairs with mincing steps, passing every object twice, barely grazing it, it and the repetitive paper like cordovan leather, trying the lights and immediately turning them off again (because they drew insects—but an observer might not be aware of this, so that, the one action countermanding the other, the whole procedure became absurd), then verifying presences and alignments by feel (surprised to find a particular vase a little too far to the left, she'd restore it to its place, she'd close a door, open a window, collect infinitesimal bits of eggshell from beneath my table, turn around [in fear of what impossible oversight?], complete her round of miniature circles). Her old age had never so moved me.

The ordinary litany of her lost ones must have formed the commentary to such agitations, for I had the thought, I who stood by idle and empty-handed, no longer daring to offer any assistance, that the old woman's omnipresence stemmed from a desperate need to fill some corresponding absence: of the son? of Desiderio? Then I remembered my own mother dead, also in a provincial bedroom, and the neighbor women and various cousins bustling around me, to spare me what tasks? what purportedly necessary laying out? (even that child of eleven—where had he come from?—who couldn't restrain himself from approaching and gently touching the corpse—whom I let do as he pleased). And I wondered, as I watched my landlady tidying things to the point of absurdity: for what corpse?

One evening, when I was feeling this discomfort more strongly than usual, I paid her, on impulse, for the month, augmented by the same sum again, which I said was a month's advance, but it was more as if I had to compensate her doubly for I-knew-not-what (as the witness of some indiscretion, perhaps: for her silence). She gave me an odd look and went away.

It happened to be the following day that I went to pick up Vanessa's photos. It's worth mentioning because I'd entertained a vague hope that the first shots would be a revelation of, or at least a clue to, the recent past of the woman I was seeing. In the interest of truth, I have to admit that I spent the whole afternoon dreaming (as I'd done before, bent over Morelle's toiletry kit, to persuade myself of we-know-what destitution) over my table on rue de Nazareth, where I'd laid out the *proofs*—as they say.

These consisted of pathetic snapshots in which the photographer's ineptitude was rivaled only by the subjects' triteness: an effect with backlit clouds, two interior scenes like those taken at birthday parties (I had difficulty recognizing her friends the Morands: the father and his little boy in the first, the mother—her head cut off—and the same son in the second), boat views of V. (the principal church, the ramparts, the palace with its row of putti, the porte des Douves Anciennes at sunset!), a fishing harbor, an ancestral portrait (from the Utopias Museum, if I was any judge, and not their finest offering—I later learned that Vanessa had seen in it some comical resemblance to one of her relatives), a completely fogged photo (me! She'd tried to take my picture with a bad flashcube while I was asleep), and the twelfth: known to us already.

When I say dreaming, I was in fact dreaming, dumb-struck before the absurdity: mine, for seeking a Desiderian meaning in such banal realities simply because they'd been *reproduced*—Vanessa's, for having memorialized them, fixed them in place, even while living them (as one might stupidly write: *I am happy* when happy, or the reverse), or for having multiplied by two, in order to preserve them, their fragility (that of the stone, of the people, plus that of the image), their wear.

Whether to indemnify myself for having spent so long fasci-nated by rubbish (I thought bitterly of Lievel) or because things had reached the point where I needed to provoke Vanessa a little more each night (in this way I measured her desire against the increasingly justified moments of rebellion it had to overcome: my own was probably contingent on it), I contrived to criticize her in a way that was half-pedantic, half-joking (but relentless, so there could be no doubt of my intention to wound) for the many faults exhibited, in my view, by her photos. (I recall that the sky was spoiled by circular lens flares. The painting's varnish haloed the portrait. Ghostly tourists truncated the columns of the principal church. And that dog! which I sneered at openly, that was looking at the bishops' residence in the foreground. The list went on . . .)

She made no reply, nor did she react in any way. And I, for my part, felt the unaccountable—and abominable, as I was well aware—need to double down. To the point that I came, that same night, to commit the entirely gratuitous act of destroying these ranging rods of the past, on the flippant grounds that they added nothing to anything and would not preserve the good days, here was the proof: I burned them one by one in the fireplace—Morand not without glee, V. as one burns one's ships, up to the twelfth (whose negative I nonetheless spared) with a strange sense of pleasure—did she see this?

How could I even attempt to justify these sacrileges? In truth, I was in such a maddened state that I asked myself, on my walks, questions such as: What forces, what fangs, am I essaying? What confession am I hoping to obtain? What in her am I trying to punish?—but instead of answering them, I found them *beautiful*. They were so many bizarre objects (for all objects are also questions): I turned them round and round in my head, and *posing* them was the final act.

It will be understood, if not pardoned, that, animated by such feelings, I was less than eager to take any action. I'd gone too far in this fantasy or caprice (I'm thinking here of the abandonment of my post, which was not a true delinquency, of the lack of method I'd shown in the case—sure that Morand would trounce me in this arena—and how many other moods and humors!) to set myself any moral imperatives now. If this caprice tended to the mortification of Vanessa C., then it must be, I thought with terrifying cynicism, that such mortification was necessary, otherwise I had

JEAN LAHOUGUE

erred from the beginning in making my desire the sole virtue of my success.

Yes, but success in what? I needed to reread the Desiderio manuscript constantly (or even: to clutch it, to thumb through its pages—actions I'm sure partook of the same pride one feels in perusing one's first book, to gauge what triumph?) to convince myself there was a mystery in it. Yet, by dint of rereading, it had become so familiar to me, was so much a part of myself, that the mystery, in fact, eluded me: it is only the Other that can be mysterious (and only others, *a contrario*, could have wondered why I'd hidden myself away, buried myself in V., for example. As far as I was concerned, I was simply staying awhile, that was all). Especially as the narrator's every act was now as self-evident to me as my own presence. Then Vanessa—I recall saying to her: "You recall . . ." in reference to a Desiderio incident we had obviously not lived ourselves, and I lost my temper because she didn't recall, because these fragments of what I believed to be my past were shared by no one, because, if worst came to worst, my entire past was doubtful: I had nothing left but anger to make me believe in it—said nothing, walked out the door, and left me.

I must now report two of these actions prosecuted against Vanessa, unjustifiable except perhaps through the species of reasoning I clung to, according to which I would never overcome a situation such as this except by an even greater, more irrevocable outrage, beyond which only tenderness, perhaps, would have satisfied me.

The first of these actions concerns the photo in which Vanessa had been caught with her thighs in a V, and which was a capital shot. I'd held onto the negative and had taken it back to the developer to have two more prints made. I have a distinct recollection of this event: the man handing me the photo envelope and giving, as his sole comment, through prudishness or embarrassment, the price, while I ostentatiously withdrew the prints, laid them on the counter, made some remark about the colors, etc., and yet even this exhibition wasn't enough for me.

As chance would have it, when I opened my wallet to pay, I found the panoramic shot of V. stolen from the Commerce the day of my arrival. It had been rather a nuisance to me since, and I had the idea to rid myself of the thing by mailing it off to some acquaintance. It was then that I thought of Lievel (if I'd ever forgotten him, for he was, to my mind, at the origin of every cupidity and every indignity, with the result that, as the trivial gradually overtook my existence in this town—recall Vanessa's idiotic photos, over which I'd pored for a full day—his image was imposing itself on me with ever greater frequency). That very evening, I sent him strange tidings indeed.

I've forgotten the exact tenor of my message, but I know I filled it with the dullest small talk that two old army buddies—which we of course were not—might exchange on the subjects of a life that was sweet and girls who were easy. As evidence of which, I know for certain that I blithely included the postcard and the obscene photo of Vanessa, without a scruple—or was it because I felt the intensest pleasure in brushing my scruples aside?

Then I carried them, these tidings, to the post office with the monumental steps, where slipping them through the slot in the wall was an act of inexpressible solemnity.

As for the other photo, I tucked it into my wallet where the postcard had been, and I remember thinking to myself, with a sort of drunken exhilaration, that if I should meet with some accident, this image would be discovered before my name.

The second of these willful infringements on Vanessa's liberty involved a search of her bag, after other similar searches. It was on a Sunday she'd been invited to the Morands—where I'd let her go by herself, naturally. In the bag, I discovered, as if they were precious artifacts, the usual makeup remover pads, as well as a used, crumpled tampon, in a paper pouch for want of a sewer drain, some keys … But most importantly, an address book containing phone numbers, which I copied into my own datebook.

The greater part of these were accompanied by a feminine first name, friends no doubt, whom I spent a long time trying to imagine, as people do in books.

It was this long list of girlfriends that had fascinated me, without my intending, at first, to make use of it. Besides, they lived in Paris, and it didn't seem that they could be in any way connected with this business. But, in the end, I conjectured that Vanessa might have taken them into her confidence regarding her internship in V., or her men. Hence the new, heinous, and preposterous step I took the following night before meeting her:

I left rue de Nazareth—I recall this ridiculous detail—with my hands in my pockets, which were full of one-franc coins: I made noise as I walked. I went to the phone booth I knew so well from having wasted my breath talking to nobody in it, just across from the Utopias Museum.

From this booth, I called all the young women from the notebook in succession. I passed myself off as the inspector and gave them to understand that Vanessa C. was mixed up in something serious. For which reason I asked them all sorts of questions about her that I'd prepared in advance, putting on an official-sounding voice. I kept my eyes on my wristwatch so as not to exceed the one-minute mark, after which the woman on the phone would realize I wasn't calling from a station office. With comical diligence I raised my voice with every coin I dropped into the slot, at regular intervals, like a responsory or an incoming tide, which even I eventually began to find droll in spite of myself, and in spite of the ignominy of the act.

They all responded with the same surprise, the same embarrassment—at any rate, this was the impression either the distance or my own agitation produced in me—if not the same voice (how could I forget that interminable collection of voices on the other end of the line, belonging to young women so thoroughly deceived that they never dared to question me!). But everything I learned from them dated from too far in the past. So that what I gained, instead of details that would have filled in my picture of Vanessa, was a sort of vertiginous disintegration or dispersion, rendering her all the more unintelligible to me.

An absurd, horrible evening it was, one that terminated, appropriately enough, with the farce of the talking clock (whose number I'd jotted down with the rest. Instead of an umpteenth young woman, I heard the time, which I had right in front of me!) since the slap in the face provided by a sense of ridiculousness was just what I needed to put an end to this folly.

Beyond which only tenderness, as I've said, would have satisfied me. And in fact I'd made a few such gestures in that direction, like those reported of certain dictators who are moved to tears over next to nothing (the death of a favorite animal, for example, and people think them good-hearted when what they're really lamenting is the bankruptcy of their own power). For what bankruptcy was I feeling my tenderness?

During this time I would wander the streets of V., and to the aforementioned series would be added the memory of the young women's voices, which expressed—as a commentary to each dog, facade, be-cigaretted shopkeeper, game animal dangling in a window, fountain, passage of children—like the numbers of my count to one hundred had before, qualifications or even doubts about Vanessa C., such as: "She had every reason, *though*, to be happy," "*but* she was so pretty," "There's *nothing* I can tell you," "I haven't heard from her in *a year*," "*two years*," "*three years*," as if all the things that multiplied themselves in V. were permutations of her flight.

Was I suffering because of this? Was I stroking all the dogs, or turning in my hands the graded fruits of a display, or feeling a silly desire to shake hands with people loitering in their doorways, in order to hold on to her? Wasn't I instead trying to cling to something, I who was maundering? The fact remains that I'd never been so distracted, or—I prefer: so absent.

Thus, it would happen that I'd suddenly quicken my pace to escape an uneasy feeling whose origin, I thought, was some house or little girl of which I'd taken too many *seconds*, as they say, and which had eventually cloyed. So much so that I was once flung, slapstick fashion, against a passerby emerging from a side street, and literally embraced him. It was several seconds before I knew why I was embracing him, if it were because I loved him or no, if I ought to release my grip. He gave me an extremely strange look.

Another time, the same befuddlement was the direct cause of a very stupid anxiety. I was walking along outdoors when I saw several motionless, perfectly mute men with their backs to me. I skirted around them but, once on the other side, there was still nothing but backs, and I had the sudden conviction, though I could see no reason for it, that this was a deliberate sign of general hostility toward me. In truth, it was quite simply a group of pétanque players intent on a deciding throw, which their very presence obscured from me. This didn't alter the fact that they'd instilled in me an extraordinary uneasiness.

And so, that evening, I loved Vanessa in a way that was like a gathering-together, the way one takes the measure of a certainty, and she said I'd gone back to being nice again. Very little time was to elapse before a new and outlandish step on my part would upset this fragile equilibrium.

IX

In reporting the events of these last weeks, I must constantly defend myself against the imputation of jealousy to which my actions—and this is not the least bizarre aspect of my liaison with Vanessa C.—will seem to lay me open in the reader's eyes, without my intending it. Not only had I persecuted her at length with questions that I myself, as I was posing them, deemed ridiculous and abominable, not only had I rifled her belongings, interrogated her friends (cross-examined, too, perhaps, to the extent that certain gentle touches can question, her body), but now, lo and behold, I had begun to follow her, hesitantly at first, and then—I deliberately employ an expression that will seem absurd—to the end.

It all started one morning when I had, unusually, risen at the same time she did. We parted company at the door of her building, but instead of going directly back to rue de Nazareth, I watched Vanessa walk away, and the loss of her felt unendurable.

As it happened, I'd never before seen her walk away from me, except at the Utopias Museum, where her disappearance had seemed quasi-miraculous, so that I found in this movement not only a resurgence of desire but also the sign that was to serve as prelude to all sorts of mysteries.

She didn't look back (likely I wouldn't have acted in the same reckless manner had she done so, for fear she might repeat the action), and, just as the curve of the street was about to swallow her, I took my first step behind her.

The road, to all appearances straight, actually bent, making Vanessa's disappearance indefinitely imminent. Imminent, too, God-knows-what explanation of the mystery I'd imagined. Guided by this interest, I would no doubt have trailed her further as early as this first day, had I not, while hugging the walls, accidentally side-swiped a pile of fruit on display (a few fruits rolled degree by degree into the gutter: I had to pick them up and apologize profusely). I could have run, but the incident had had a sobering effect on me.

On the following mornings, nevertheless, I gave in to the same temptation, prolonging my surveillance by a few buildings or streets, but without daring to bring it to term (either because, to my mind, this renunciation absolved me of whatever there was of the dishonorable in my proceedings, or because, unbeknownst to me, I was growing accustomed—how could I have been blind to this possibility, which would have seemed so unbearable then?—to separating from Vanessa a little later each time, to gauge, perhaps, my privation). It took an additional chance occurrence to over-come my scruples.

In the meantime, I wasn't jealous, and only my Desiderio curiosity gave the impression that I was, but it was so strong an impression that at the end of all my posturing it seemed Desiderio must be the object of a jealousy to come.

And so I didn't dare follow Vanessa as far as I might have, since I had all the time in the world—as they say—until the day when, having read her an episode from the Desiderio manuscript, her face authorized me to commit any and all abuses.

The passage in question was the one in which the narrator, walking his index and middle fingers in tiny steps across the *Belle Dame*'s body, draws up a sort of inventory, coat of arms, or topology of the same, in a vocabulary that exasperated Vanessa because it was identical to that of her work, and she was sick of it.

She used this story as a pretext for the fiercest criticisms she had yet leveled at me concerning Desiderio—the most minor of which being that he was more or less participating in our love-making! But that which should have opened my eyes seemed to me, by its very violence, to be so unjust that my scruples—those that had checked me that morning, at the moment when I'd once again chosen the Vanessa mystery over its imminent resolution—vanished.

On that day, therefore, I followed Vanessa all the way to the end: the ponderous classical building that formed a triangle with the main post office and the police station. She was finishing up some work there having to do with the town (a dissertation, she'd told me—and either she'd left me in the dark or I'd stopped listening—which was supposed to legitimize some silly, artificial internship) and all the more so now that its language and Desiderio's had coincided to such a degree that they'd become the object of a single anger.

I stood idly awhile, arms dangling, in front of the long administrative building that served as town hall, tourist bureau, and probably many other things besides, as if seeing it sufficed to grasp it, and all the actions and desires it had shaped along with it, I thought. An orderly of some kind was approaching me, so I decided to enter resolutely and avoid the necessity of speaking to him.

The lobby, at the top of the steps, was papered with flyers and circulars. It was surprisingly cool. An arrow on a floor stand struck me as whimsically absurd because it directed the visitor, when he was scarcely through the front door, to exit out the back (I later learned it was pointing toward the registry office across the court-yard, but it might have been the street). Typewriter sounds could be heard.

The orderly's eyes weighing heavily on me, I went through the first door on my left, where I'd seen the words "Lending Library": this was a large room lined with books, with an isolated desk at which a woman of indeterminate age—with an indeterminate glance in my direction—was sorting unbelievably grubby-looking catalog cards.

(Here, I recall a disagreeable sensation: Having nothing to ask the woman, I turned decisively toward the shelves and stumbled, thanks to the accidents of a classification system I suppose was alphabetical, on one title, then another, then at least ten more, all of which contained the same word—it was *music*—followed by the names of countries, by *in the church*, *for the theater*, *numbered notation*, *for voice*, etc., as if there was nothing in the world but that, music, or rather as if, chance ruling all, I couldn't possibly have wanted anything else: I felt smothered. Ridiculously, the tune of *My Blue Heaven* came back to me.) I moved on to other rooms.

I visited many, all equally long and forbidding, where no one addressed a single question to me. Just as I was about to give up hope, I entered one that I knew immediately, from its posters (which showed the town's main points of interest—the Utopias, for example) and tourist brochures, to be the right one. There was a receptionist behind a counter, to whom I said that I was passing through V. and wanted to see the sights.

What I decided next, setting in motion that day's dramatic events, and which I had in no way planned and is incomprehensible to me even now, so surpasses the essential indolence of my nature that I beg the reader to ready his indulgence one last time—provided my attitude of these last few weeks hasn't already condemned me in his eyes.

My original intention had been to thank the receptionist for the brochures and group-tour passes she'd offer me, then express anxiety about a friend of mine named Vanessa C. (I guessed that her workspace must be right there, in the rooms with ranges of archives I could see over the receptionist's shoulder). I'd go and surprise her amid this griminess, and it seemed to me, in some obscure way, that seeing her thus would have pleased me.

But my little white lie, concerning my alleged desire to see the sights of a town I already knew like the back of my hand, brought to mind a piece of information someone had told me about Morelle: he'd occasionally served as a tour guide, having a thorough knowledge of the arts. Giving in to this impetus, I asked the receptionist eagerly (on some pretext or other—I couldn't read a map, I needed to talk to someone about my pleasures—that merely emphasized the suspect nature of my request: I realized this as soon as the words were out of my mouth) whether it would be possible for me to be *escorted*. I was received with a look, first of stupefaction, then of marked reproach.

I persevered. I insisted that a friend of mine, Morelle, had—in this very town—taken visitors around, that such a thing must necessarily be done, that I was prepared to pay whatever the asking price, the proof: I flung onto the counter, in a fit of true madness (but one which might still be taken as the whim of a very wealthy traveler), all the cash I had on me.

"I don't know," stammered the receptionist. "I'll have to ask Monsieur ***, but I'm sure you're mistaken."

She returned, followed by a man to whom I repeated my request as calmly as I could. He listened to me with a serious demeanor (it was affected, I believe, and appeared almost comical in relation to the outlandish role in which I'd cast myself). Then:

"We don't offer guided tours of the town during the off-season," he said, "except for community groups who've put in a request in advance. Your friend may have been one of the students we use in such cases. His name doesn't ring a bell . . ."

He smiled.

"You can always find, on the streets of V., some boy who'll take you around to the major landmarks for a coin or two. But I doubt his commentary will be of the sort to satisfy you. I'm very sorry . . ."

Probably my eyes were on the back rooms at this moment. Seeing which, my interlocutor must himself have thought of Vanessa, said "unless," and disappeared.

I heard his voice and hers (while the receptionist and I, on our side of the wall, stared at each other in silence). When they returned, I was no longer sure what I wanted. Vanessa was disconcerted by my request, and by my coming there. But she didn't give me away, and I played my role through to the end, trying to make her comprehend by my performance that my object was to liberate her for the day (I had no way out apart from this thoughtfulness!), amid the greatest confusion.

It was agreed that Mademoiselle C. would escort me through V. The unaccustomed sum, which did not figure on any price list (I didn't want to take any of it back), would go to God-knows-what conservation society defending against wind and sea. That was how it all began.

All, meaning: the inconceivable circuit of V. we made under Vanessa's guidance (by way of explanation, if not of excuse, there was something ambiguous about my offer from the start, stemming from the fact that Vanessa's acceding to such an odd and dubious desire on the part of a stranger must have made her seem like I-don't-know-what, so that this gift of a day, paid for as a trick, was also a public insult—did we feel this?) though we should have laughed off the idea, since, after all, we'd been laughing up our sleeves at the receptionist and the man without needing to confer. We were out on the steps with a day's vacation ahead of us.

Yet I affirmed to Vanessa that I did, in fact, want to see the town's sights, *since that's what I'd paid for.* What's more, I heard myself pronouncing this absurd and ignoble demand with a certain jauntiness, as if under cover of a joke that would be kept going a little while longer—to the bottom of the steps, then to the street corner, in order to deceive any possible surveillance, and then beyond—for no reason whatsoever.

Vanessa, to begin with, played along with this game that wasn't a game. I remember she gave me a presentation, in a very loud voice and with a sunny smile, on the ponderous classical building that formed a triangle with the main post office and the police station, while passersby stumbled a little as they came near the bizarre couple we formed, because they were expecting a lovers' spat and what they got instead was art talk. But as the joke, for want of any justification, began to wear thin, I saw her growing tense.

Little by little, we let ourselves be drawn into the horrible one-upmanship of pointless questions and acerbic answers about the old walls, still acting out the tourist-visit gag, without knowing, either of us, whether we should have one last laugh about it or not, or simply take to our heels and flee. And so I would demand the history of such-and-such a building and Vanessa, in the same parodic tone, would say that it was the Hotel X., give the keys to interpreting two or three symbolic ornaments, then quickly segue into saying that it was here she'd known her first lover (then her second, then her *n*th, as we went from old edifice to old edifice), focusing—did she think that in doing so she was setting some sort of jealousy at defiance?—in coarser and coarser language, such as I'd never known her to use, on her body's successive awakenings to unheard-of perversions, me nodding along like a tourist, snapping pictures to record some imaginary scandal, and asking still more questions.

Or, further on, when swarms of children cut across our path, she'd cry out that all of them (it occurred to me that these were potential guides, and that each, for a pittance, might have submitted their own lies about V. to me, and I might have chosen the finest) were her sons, abandoned on all the doorsteps in town, and other lunacies, so loudly that people were looking at us, us, the walls, and the children, with such imbecile expressions that we had fresh reasons to laugh (or not), and to continue.

Of this mad game (one of those destined to end late at night, on I-know-not-what irreparable bust) I must here report three moments (or places?) whose painful recollection is more deeply engraved on my memory.

The first was when we were on the parvis of the principal church. The statues in their niches were eroded (the sea wasn't far off, and the V. mesa was the first obstacle that confronted the wind).

Vanessa was speaking more and more loudly. The tourists at the base of the steps had equally good views of both us and the exceptional facade with its mutilated gods. I felt an indescribable embarrassment which, out of pride, I didn't want to bring to an end, and I dutifully responded with the vociferous and stupid exaltations required.

Then Vanessa undertook to round out this chronicle with her own commentary, still as if addressing a crowd. I listened in alarm as she imputed to the saints, whose attitudes of prayer had been lost, acts of the most provocative obscenity (she turned the ardor still visible in their faces to her own ends), and swelled the members beneath the habits eaten away by time. As for me, I retreated step by step with exclamations of "Ah!" as if I were backing up to take a picture, but perhaps—in truth—to distance myself from her, or was it to oblige her to say *those things* at even greater volume?

Later. We were walking alongside the bishops' residence. I pushed, or nearly pushed, Vanessa into the Utopias Museum, where we had our share of memories. Maybe I needed to obliterate them with other, *contrary* memories, because I incited her to further expansion and development of her theme. But what she offered me surpassed my most sordid secret wishes, everything being for her a pretext for filth.

This is not the place to report her words in all their excess. They echoed through the galleries, and I was cowardly enough, without altogether breaking character, to interrupt her ten times or more with questions that were less scurrilous—on art or history, for example—probably because that ludicrous guard had appeared and was visibly wavering over whether to consider each new statement a depredation, an act of plunder. But then she would finish her speech with a smile whenever it became too flagrantly objectionable, so that I myself didn't know whether or not we were deliberately provoking the man.

And it was only once evening had fallen, after we'd been down all the main thoroughfares, driven on by our own foolishness, and had repulsed, because we were too proud, every temptation to beg each other's pardon, that, almost by accident, the decisive event took place.

It was as we were passing in front of the house I've called the town's cunt. Once again, I demanded that Vanessa provide expository remarks. But this time, while I awaited the false avowal of fresh depravities (but was she enjoying this game as much as I supposed?) she turned on me with all the insults she had hitherto been heaping on the third parties in our comedy, ceding to me by the same act (I nonetheless felt an odd sense of relief under this rain of profanity) what hollow victory?

Then she went quiet, and I followed her in silence to rue de Palaevouno. On the landing—I was about to go in after her—Vanessa told me no, she'd had an exhausting day's work.

What else could she have said?

Such were my bitterest memories, among a thousand others, of that awful day on which I'd gradually driven my girlfriend, from pointless explanation to pointless exposition, into speaking the words of our first falling-out.

I was still reeling from the blow, and my landlady's chatter struck me as utterly empty and trivial. (I remember she was less and less often, it seemed, touching small objects and the *cartapesta* of the walls. I thought to myself that she couldn't have failed to see the two of us around V., which we'd explored from top to bottom, that she wanted to draw a confession from me and was being gentle because all confessions are born of gentleness. But I would have preferred her to take things firmly in hand and was crushing them in my breast. She steered the conversation toward her childhood, I suppose for the same reason.)

I was listening to her as I would to music, meaning: mindful chiefly of the repetitions and variations, and these were numerous, as they are with all old ladies (the subjects were her grandmother's house; an orange tree in the back garden—from one of its oranges [she said this in passing: because I myself had picked one up in order that I might tear the skin off something] she'd fashioned the belly of a little man with very long hands, which she'd loved, and which had rotted, and had been thrown in the trash for, so she said, moral reasons: she'd wept over it—; Ascension Day with its altars of repose, which she used to recreate in miniature in her room— out of piety, or for fun?; her girlfriends, who would go to the *** beach completely covered up; the chains they used to make from seashells; and I forget what else …) while I tried to recall what Vanessa had said, and of course could recall nothing but the walls.

It seemed that all was lightness with my landlady, and that she was robbing me of my tragedy. Even down to her glances, which were *sidelong*, lacking in depth (in fact, I quickly realized—it was quite silly—she was doing this to look for fingerprints, or water rings, against the light. But the impression remained). I would have liked to shoo her out. Then I reproached myself, of course.

I believe that, above all, these frailties on rue de Nazareth (my landlady's, who in speaking of her childhood had never seemed so old; mine, because at first I wanted to smash everything to pieces and a second later felt moved to tears of pity), as well as the fact that the sorrow of a breakup often has to do with the *remains* (and Madame Vian had never extended a hand toward that vase, for example, without deferring by as much my nightly reunion with Vanessa, so that I'd never rejoined Vanessa except *against* this gesture and *against* this vase) revealed to me the enormity of my conduct.

At that moment, I was seized with a passionate desire to repair the damage, and perhaps I would have run to rue de Palaevouno on the instant if not, indeed, for the old woman. But as she droned on, as the walls of V. passed before me in memory, marked one and all by the aforementioned obscenities, which were the scattered emblems of our discord, the certainty came upon me that no forgiveness could be practiced in V. and that flight was the only option.

Would that I had carried this design, too, through to the end, instead of confining myself—as they stupidly say—to what was right next door (would I have felt I was derelict in some arbitrary Desiderio duty if I'd taken the train back to Paris with Vanessa by any means possible? Was the desire of the entirely covered-up young women dictating that I go to the neighboring bay of *** and no other? At any rate, does one ever truly flee?): the sea!

For I instantly conceived the timid and vulgarly prosaic plan of taking Vanessa to the seaside to wipe the slate clean. Did my landlady understand this as she gazed at me mournfully, as if I'd given up on something?

I waited until Sunday. I'd hired a car for the day. I went to meet Vanessa at her place and knocked, for once. I begged her to forget that horrible day of narrated houses, of pockmarked gods, and give me a second chance.

She listened to my proposition in silence (in fact, she began to walk about the room, picking up whatever came to hand, a record, a bottle of ambergris, and putting it down again in the same motion, in the nervous way one sometimes does before making an important decision, and I had the baroque idea that she was successively depriving my words, like the bottle and the record, of their object—in short: that there would be none left. Finally, she made an unintentional gesture that seemed wondrous to me by contrast—without opening it, she pressed the porcelain knob of the entry door—and which was already a sign of assent). Then she fastened her bag, slung it over her shoulder, and smiled.

The morning was enchanting. Once past the railroad bridge (it marked, in my mind, the boundary of V., because I'd never ventured beyond it) the air was finer. There were trees (extraordinary, in my view, and I was surprised at being so moved by them—then I recalled that there were no trees within the town walls), fields ravaged by the wind: I can still see Vanessa's hand, outstretched through the window and opened in the direction of our travel, above them.

The one and only road led to ***, the harbor, and the seafront already mentioned. In the off-season it was almost deserted. Three out of every four shops were closed, with flyers and handbills (people were trying to unload anything and everything, from a pair of sandals to a flower-filled villa on the bay) pasted on the shutters.

I still remember the terns, the innumerable painters we had to step over, the corresponding number of fishing boats tilted on their bellies at various angles, the tide having ebbed (I even remember photographing one, which Vanessa found more picturesque than the others for God-knows-what reason, almost aground in the mud with the jetty behind it, but lovingly and without malice this time, to efface, I suppose, the memory of the parodic photos from the other day), and the long series of their maidenly names.

There was a restaurant at one end of the harbor where, somewhat childishly, we decided to eat nothing but seafood.

It was afternoon by the time I took Vanessa out onto the strand of ***. This follows the incomplete circle of a bay whose colors were nonetheless delightful. A mist hung over the water, though the sky was clear. There was almost no one on the beach, and I told her it was all ours. Only, near the tideway and well back from the sea, some children were fashioning a boat from mud and stones, with undersized sails that made papery sounds and raised a smile.

There were seashells, too, and I said, in a loud voice because we were practically alone, that I had seashells at my place, in Paris, and other inanities. I collected a few. I tried my hand at identification. (Until we came to a whitish, gooey octopus that had washed up on the sand, at which Vanessa made a face because she'd almost stepped on it, and which filled me with a strange unease.) Until there were no more shells: we no longer needed to speak.

We walked out toward the water, and I was already thinking our agonizing week had been forgotten. One might well smile at this naivete, and at the comical figure I must have cut, barefoot and carrying my dress shoes (now that I think of it: to prevent what noise? To avoid disturbing what happiness, to surprise what truth or flee what trap?). Vanessa was letting her bag trail along the ground, which drew something between us.

When we were at the edge of the water (I remember I stayed two steps behind Vanessa, because of a silly detail that was not enough to spoil the whole—I laughed it off: the trousers of my dress suit, whereas for my companion's bare legs the edge was further out), I experienced a sense of miraculous equilibrium that, even today, stupid author of its flight or plaything of misfortune, I desperately interrogate.

The sea was perfectly calm. Between two of the tiny wavelets that were rolling in with strange regularity and burying themselves behind us in the sand, one (but who?) would have thought we'd been set atop a hard, glassy surface on which our reflections were nearly intact. I was struck by the thought that Morand was awaiting bodies from this same sea, the feeling of being ridiculous, and a delicious, childish thrill of anxiety. In the suddenness of our departure, we naturally hadn't brought bathing attire. Then, at an imperceptible movement of Vanessa's, I was sure we were both envisaging, in synchronicity, a nakedness that had nothing to do with desire, more ambiguous perhaps.

Did I think it unlikely that this temptation could have come from me? Was I imagining, in all seriousness, the aforementioned *one* who might have been watching us from afar, in some suspect state of patient expectation? I turned around at that precise instant, and all my joy seemed to turn to scorn.

A man was, in fact, standing there in the middle of the beach. Without justification. Facing us. Stunned, I noted his shabby suit, the glasses on his forehead (I thought of someone who'd been torn away from the placid perusal of a newspaper so he'd have to look further afield—and indeed he was holding something that might have been taken for a paper: in truth, a road map), I wanted to laugh.

Then I remembered my shadowers, whom all sorts of intoxicating exhilarations had made me forget. And I heard myself say to Vanessa these unfortunate, and very unfair, words: "Here's your protector!" (I think, or "protégé!") which was nothing, as I saw it, but a means of driving off the pest.

I'd spoken so he would hear, and the man didn't insist. At least, he walked off to the left with the air of someone setting out to cover kilometers of shoreline. Vanessa made no comment, offered no reflections. She led me away from the water toward the row of cabins, but there was no longer any question of going nude, or of anything else.

However, she did ask me to wait there and took the keys to go and fetch bathing gear, she said, from the car. (I was surprised, but wrongly surprised. What I mean is: something serious had occurred which apparently ruled out any water sports, and this was why her intentions seemed surprising to me. The truth was, I *knew* Vanessa had brought nothing with her but her bag, whose contents I could recite by heart, in her excitement.)

I waited for perhaps a quarter of an hour, sitting in the sand, obsessing over the something I was letting slip through my fingers, but unable to tell whether this something was merely a singular detail (for example: the cabins curving away in long perspectives to the right and left, as if reflecting each other—I mention it because this single concrete memory dogs me), a Desiderio revelation, or my chance.

The car wasn't far off. I'd intuitively fixed a deadline for Vanessa's return. Once it had passed, exactly when, according to either reason or need, she should have reappeared, I heard a patter of footsteps behind me, no doubt joyous, and saw a group of three young women burst out from between the cabins. They were in bathing suits, and were strapping and vulgar, such that right away, their breasts and enormous thighs attracting my eye, I felt a violent surge of desire for them.

It was only then that I understood Vanessa's transparent lie, and that she had fled. When, out of breath, I regained the seaside promenade, the car had disappeared.

Such was the pitiable story of the day at *** that could have been so pleasant, and that I'd ruined in all innocence. I was annoyed with myself. I was annoyed with Vanessa for her subterfuge. I was annoyed with the stranger who was at the root of it all and was laughing—this I was prepared to swear, stranded amid the rows of extravagant villas and shrubbery—at my distress (it may seem ridiculous that my first feeling was in fact one of distress, an infantile terror at finding myself without papers, so I thought, without money, without anyone I knew). The rest is of little interest.

I had some difficulty getting a car to stop in the thickening fog and give me a ride. I was so shaken by events that on several occasions I became convinced we were being followed, and I pointed out to the driver as proof the pair of headlights in our rear window. To which he complacently replied that people always drove bumper-to-bumper in such fog, and that he himself wasn't letting the lights ahead of us out of his sight. He must have thought I'd been reading too many novels, judging from his smile.

In V. I found my car in the fountain square. A reflector had been smashed in I-never-knew-what crack-up—me, I thought! I didn't go to rue de Palaevouno that night, or any of the nights that followed.

X

There seemed nothing to indicate, while so many things, my love itself, were slipping from my grasp, that I'd ever reach a successful conclusion one day, and yet there was: I had confidence like never before, because all these things resumed, once removed from my use—though it would more aptly be called *abuse*—, a state of self-evident facticity, and this fact struck me in return. I was saying to myself *Vanessa C.* and no longer *she*, for example, Vanessa C. being clearer, paradoxically, when I was choosing not to know her (which of course I also mean in the sexual sense). But it was primarily in a spirit of irony that I placed, in the hours following the trip to ***, such weight on the Desiderio case, and in desperation that I repeated to myself, as in popular novels, that I was "at that stage of the investigation where, confusedly, the pieces were beginning to fall into place and the finished picture to emerge."

In truth, my first impulse was to write to Vanessa. I imagined a brief letter, free from literary pretensions, in which I would show that my desire to understand, at all costs, my correspondent's disappearance and the strange events of my stay, was entirely legitimate. From which desire, in my opinion, stemmed those tactless blunders she might have taken the wrong way, such as the unfortunate words applied to the man I'd mentally dubbed the voyeur of the bay, whom I would demonstrate by cross-references to have numbered among my swarm of stalkers (but I struck out *swarm*—as overly melodramatic: this was certainly not the goal—and substituted: *my informers*), the scabrous tour of V., etc.

But it turned out that this letter, in the first place, was extremely long, and then itself accumulated schoolboy blunders, misusages, and above all a remarkable amount of drift (I even had the alarming thought that it was taking me back to the vicious circles of my youth: I would write something, and then, the spirit being no longer the same after five or six pages, I'd have to start the story over from the beginning, rewrite the whole thing, watch it take on fresh distortions, and redo it once again), so that after three disastrous attempts, I gave it up.

I ascribed to fatigue, and to the fact that this incident still struck too close to home for me to speak about it well, this inability to keep my dogs leashed. But it brought with it a singular consequence of which I did not immediately appreciate the gravity or the tragicomic implications, and which I must here describe: It gradually came to pass that the very idea of my relations with Vanessa seemed ungraspable, that, over and above Vanessa, the least of my desires in some sense smacked of the implausible as soon as it arose (and I began thinking to myself absurdities more or less along the lines of: "No! it's not possible that I wish to press my body against the wall to feel the coolness" or "to drink milk" or "to *know* this or that beautiful woman passing beneath the window on rue de Nazareth that I now never leave"), in so extraordinarily compelling a fashion that, in effect, nothing tempted me anymore.

When I was a child, every now and then my mother would enjoin me to sudden immobility and silence because there was a bird, a handsome peacock butterfly, or some entirely different presence within a range of several meters around us. Much later, as chance would dictate during my games with other children, it would sometimes happen that I'd stop dead in my tracks, or at least prolong for no reason (the why, the circumstances of the maternal order completely escaping me) some movement promising to cause a racket, under this lone imperative to immobility and silence.

My desire was now paralyzed in the same way. My essential daily activities (I no longer went out except to eat and, in the afternoons, smoked I don't know how many packs of Gauloises) created a sort of neutral space around me, and it was there, seemingly, in that void, where I was doing nothing but repeating the word *denouement* to myself (though whether I was thinking of Vanessa or the investigation I couldn't say), that the boundaries and abuttals of the finished picture I spoke of began to take shape.

One of the rare breaches in my vacuity, specifically a chance occurrence at one of those meals I ate out—the idea of dining alone or preparing my own food not being very appealing to me—occasioned an incident worth the telling, as it inadvertently furnished me (but I was to understand this only at length) with a key piece of evidence.

It was one week to the day after the misadventure of the bay. An idle fancy came into my head to dine at the Palazzo rather than at the Commerce, where I'd fallen into the habit of having a single course and dessert. It was a mad extravagance, because I was starting to run low on funds and would be squandering there, in one hour, three days of ordinary existence. But there was no *ordinary existence* anymore, and I was fully capable of making the unconscious and suicidal calculation according to which, being more quickly deprived of resources, I'd be forced to search elsewhere, in another way, perhaps a more adventurous and inspired way, for the who and what of events. Furthermore, though there was nothing in this fantasy that could have, directly or indirectly, suggested the idea, so pharisaical, of a pilgrimage, I must have had some notion that a fortuitous encounter at the Palazzo, where Vanessa and I had, I naively thought, *exchanged names*, was the only miracle now capable of expunging so many mistakes.

One glance around the large dining room already known to the reader, with its mirrors and draperies, cured me of all illusions on this score. There were a dozen or so exaggeratedly quiet customers: a family, a table of young women—Vanessa not among them—, a few lone men—commercial travelers, I'd guess, from their leather briefcases and the files they were poring over—, and two senior citizens. I sat down unthinkingly at the table we'd occupied before, and my attention was engaged for a while in passing in review—as we so justly say—everything that lent itself to remembrances (the border pattern, to begin with, that ran as ever around the walls and lamps—turned off, as it so happened—, the line of uniformed servers: I saw their reflected hands knotted behind their backs in a mirror, the heavy tiebacks, all trappings—I thought ironically—of what they call bygone splendor) until this tender feeling, as if suddenly transformed, became a veritable pain.

It was then that I saw Morand. He was sitting almost directly in front of me. It was he who was the father of the aforementioned family to which I'd paid such scant attention, either because it had seemed inconceivable that I might know any family here, or because—more simply—the inspector had had his back to me at the time. But now he was staring hard at me with such an expression that not for an instant did it cross my mind to go over and greet him, him or his wife, nor even to make a sign of friendly recognition.

Rattled at first by his attitude, I presently came to find it amusing, as an example of petty meanness very much in keeping with his character (he must have suspected me still of encroaching on his territory), and even made so bold as to feign as much impudent curiosity about his table as he was showing about mine.

And so I told myself that today must be either the maid's day off or a Sunday outing promised to the kiddies, which nauseated me, and which gave me unlimited license by helping me to cast Morand as vulgar—despite his airs—and I applied myself to the task of making my thoughts known. His wife, of whom I'd seen only a glimpse on rue des Douves Anciennes and her cut-off head in Vanessa's photo, had a thick, obscene neck, and I could see nothing—would never see anything—but her neck. The little boy, now totally ignored by his father, was eating with his hands some sort of disgusting pap that left a snotlike ring around his mouth. The little girl was sculpting a creature out of fruit, spittle, and crumbs that her parents were trying to snatch away from her with half-hearted grabs, aborted because they wanted to conceal them from the servers and other diners—she was defending it like her own flesh and blood. Not a word was spoken by any of them. I thought it was the most pitiful sight I'd ever seen.

I must have been smiling already, and even, without meaning to, through force of observation, more or less imitating them, for example by vigorously rubbing my fingers together, soiled by some imaginary stickum, pointedly mashing up my food—the most refined and expensive on the menu, as much from a spirit of unconscious provocation as to burn my ships—or wiping at great length, for no apparent reason, my entire face up to the forehead.

At the end of the meal, I watched the wife lead away her silent, dumbfounded children. Once they were gone, Morand approached me and seated himself unceremoniously at my table for two, in the place, I thought, that belonged to Vanessa, my love, and I was resentful. But he was furious. At first I thought it was my mimicry, but none of what he proceeded to spit in my face (that my very presence made him sick, that I ought to be locked up, bastard that I was and God-knows-what else, that he'd given me fair warning and now couldn't care less about what I had coming—he promised me it would be one for the books!) was related to that, I felt sure, and I was still groping for what it was all about when he literally bolted out the door.

The whole scene had lasted scarcely a minute. I realized I'd been smiling rather stupidly the whole time—as a defensive measure, no doubt. My hand was in the air. The young women were looking at me. The lone men too, probably, over their folios. The line of servers was as before. I paid and left.

The incident tormented me all that week, my last, during which I continued to spend everything I had hand over fist, with the additional reason, now, that V.'s rare places of entertainment might provide an opportunity to cross paths once again with the inspector, who was at the end of his tether and could not fail to say—according to a marvelous expression—*too much*.

I was convinced, after his outburst, that Morand's involvement in this affair went beyond his role as a mere representative of law and order—events would soon bear me out—and so my thoughts ran—perhaps because there was the sea and he was expecting so much from it—to a traffic in I-knew-not-what, of which he was the center—or, in a manner less childishly romantic and more plausible, given his position and his temptations as a man on the make, in influence, as they say. But on this point I had gone completely astray.

Perhaps I'd even been hoping to meet a Vanessa as unoccupied, as unjustified as I was in these places I've described as *of entertainment* (which was something of a joke, because I could have searched V. in vain for a wine-tasting cellar or a gaming circle: one miserable movie house, the theater . . .), but V. was still too big to run across the same woman twice purely by chance—it was a utopia.

At any rate, these evenings out were convenient in that they delivered me from my landlady, who was growing ever more restless and taciturn as time wore on, and as I kept putting into her hands, with prodigal liberality, the price of the coming months, as if I were still buying her silence—but silence on the matter of what follies?—while everything continued, for her and for me, as it had in those happy evenings of my love when I would slip away to rue de Palaevouno just at the theater hour, as it happened.

At that hour I could no longer see the facades with their unpleasant memories, or else I saw them altered under the floodlights, under the insect-clouds that were pulverizing, for example, the saints of the principal church—I believed in them less. And I told myself, on my way, that whatever moronic drama they were showing at the municipal theater, or B movie at the movie house, which I would adore for the space of an evening because it was simple, because one could immediately see which corner God was in and which the Devil, would by the same token be the means of escaping my burgeoning anxiety by stamping Vanessa's flight (or worse) with the mark of childishness.

In truth, I saw no more than two shows, and with cause: things were not like they were during the season. The first was a children's adventure (I remember the worn-out soundtrack, the endless intermission when bags were left on seats while people went off to drink, urinate, or smoke—and I, to pass the time, traced the contours of my face with my joined fingertips), the other was a melodrama complete with missives, poison, traitors lurking in the shadows, tragic cases of mistaken identity, and scenery on wheels, part of the X. tour circuit (the very red hall in the Italian style, the elderly subscription holders in the orchestra section, where I was, occupying the most expensive seats, the young people up above who tossed a paper airplane. But over and above everything else, the ridiculous incident with my only young neighbor, who laughed at nothing and shuddered at nothing, who was, in short, even more conspicuously an outsider than I was, with a face so grave and handsome that I had a maniacal urge to talk to him, presently, and even—this was outrageous—to touch his hand, until he suddenly sprang up and threw off his disguise, pushing past me as though I'd never existed, and rushed the stage with ten other brigands to slay the prince, a supernumerary!)—and every time I turned around, in the hope that one or the other of the people I sought had come in during the intermission, I saw nothing but a frightful row of heads that were detached, in the light of the screen or stage, from the surrounding darkness, absolutely pallid.

Afterward, passing through the lobbies (I would have been sure, in Paris, to run into a hundred-odd friends there: the place itself made my heart swell with longing to see them), I recognized no one, so emphatically no one that all the people facing me seemed the reverse of friends, deliberately dragging me, so I thought, into the jostling throng.

Both times, I stood dazed on the edge of the sidewalk under a street lamp, annoyed with the absent in general, with Vanessa who hadn't felt the same desire I had, now reviled, with the dispersing audience, ugly old folks and children, or nearly so, to whom I would have had, in the manner that appeals to former hooligans (I speak of this as of a childish and contemptible temptation that actually did come over me in my rage), in order to detain them or see their eyes, to furtively flash that photo I no longer possessed of Vanessa in an obscene pose—a temptation that soon lost its power, since, like them, the old folks and the children, I would have barely smiled at the miserable wretch and continued on my way. It was so very late.

At this rate, by Sunday morning I had no more to my name than the price of a light meal at the Commerce, if that. I would have just enough left to telegram a request for assistance to the *** Press—for lack of somewhere more glorious—in the early hours of Monday— they'd grant me that, surely I still had some rights—and I would eat, in the meantime, the oranges I'd saved until then because they looked nice in the baskets.

I took longer than usual over this meal. Perhaps because I wasn't exactly enchanted with the idea of returning to my big house, bigger each day as I grew poorer, more incapable of possessing it, or even—at each audit of my finances, I mean: all that my senses perceived there, in the way of signs, confirming my dispossession—of preserving my right to its use. I made a meal, too, of my idle evening on rue de Nazareth, through my experience of an earlier day-after-a-show for one, when everything had turned out to be the opposite of an action, of a surprise, of a possible exchange with someone on the way out, of a way out, and on which I'd nonetheless had no end of trouble falling asleep, for having risen too late that morning.

After which, I lingered for another hour or so, listening to absurd disagreements litigated by rounds of bellowing, watching the billiard players, who numbered two—their heads lost in the shadows of the back room while their hands were extraordinarily luminous—as if each shot, long calculated and awaited, marked one more step in a decipherable progression, and soothed me. (At the same time, this didn't prevent my abstracting, from the spinning rack on my left, a new panorama of V., like on that first day, with the justification, however, that the need to take away an image of V. that was also an image of theft had become urgent.)

When I was finally on my way back up rue de Nazareth, all the beauties of the facades, *tempietto* or stele, that I saw, as when I'd counted to one hundred, had numbers assigned to them against my will, and I could no longer tell if they were those of the billiard game prolonged to infinity, a childish method of inducing sleep or forgetfulness, or a tally of ignominious lovers such as that of which

I nursed a bitter recollection. It was at the end of this uncontrollable and absurd enumeration that I saw Vanessa.

I was late, then—but for what rendezvous that had never been set?—and she'd had to wait a long time for me, in the middle of the street in front of number 11, arms at her sides, looking lost and weary, so that anyone's first thought would have been to render her aid of some kind, or to ask her all sorts of concerned questions—me, I had plenty of things to ask her, but what? her presence was clearly the answer to all of them. I could only say come inside . . . She came inside.

She'd never been to my place, because for obscure reasons I'd rejected the idea out of hand, and because we'd gotten used to rue de Palaevouno with its crowded landing.

During the few minutes following our entry, during which neither she nor I could find words, our only exchange arose from symbolic, slightly ridiculous gestures, me showing, she discovering, at least the two rooms of the ground floor—the long, sparse furnishings, the wallpaper with its sprays—silently, as if to obliterate the commentary of another tour.

She turned and touched, that evening, everything, but only barely, with her fingertips, just enough, so it seemed, to confirm the objects' existence (which I was beginning to doubt—but had there ever been anything besides that, objects?—ever since I had become poor and powerless to preserve them, starting—there was cause here to smile—with my oranges), except one orange, as it happened, which she picked up to contravene this gentleness, to have a reason to still not speak, and pressed.

She also opened the cupboards and reclosed them, my suitcase and reclosed it, unfolded the towels my landlady, who did my laundry, had brought back in my absence, and replaced them.

I recalled, seeing her, the neighbor women and cousins who never managed to tell me my mother was going to die, there in the upstairs bedroom, who touched everything, either to justify this silence or to give me, through the spectacle of intense and somber activity, the illusion that every effort was being made to reverse the evil, that there was nothing to fear. (What death, then, did Vanessa have to conceal from me? And what strange temptation did I feel to go up to the bedroom with her and secure for myself what peace of mind?)

When she did speak, it was almost a question, something parenthetical—she'd thought I was gone, she said—because no categorical statements were to be made that evening (but this had in fact been true for a long while, since the day of those memories that are also almost questions). I replied that I almost was, that I'd spent quite a lot since the other Sunday. *** wouldn't turn a blind eye to such irresponsibility forever and would pull my chestnuts out of the fire one last time only on the condition that I return to rue de H., which was the wisest course. And yet I'd gone to the theater only yesterday, to the movies another time, I'd been thinking of her, in short it was still questions, disordered questions, spoken with a sort of timidity because I suspected that this was a moment of equilibrium, precious and precarious.

We talked on in this way for a long while, our voices low, me feeling tempted time and again to broach more openly what must have been the sole subject close to our hearts: us, now (as when she put money on the table—for the photos, she said—the moment having thus come to either say no or else close my eyes to this kind attention with what could only be a view toward once again pooling our resources, but I didn't protest), and prevented immediately each time by I-know-not-what imperative to immobility and silence. But one can never speak for long about nothing.

Was it only by chance, and because, amid the mass of minor events from the last fifteen days that were furnishing grist for this peripheral conversation, on the margins of ourselves, and almost happy, it was impossible for me to forget this particular one? Was it, on the contrary, that I was deliberately dwelling on this event, already aware (washing my hands of my clearest interests, lucid after my own fashion) of the consequences of such a remembrance, accepting them as necessary—but what was this monstrous necessity that impelled me to do the unpardonable, as if there were no enjoyment except in the impossibility of atonement? It will seem quite extraordinary that I should be incapable of teasing out the role of my own will in an incident so serious and so recent (and yet, who among us ever knows what directs our intentions or our words?), but I wound up giving a detailed account of the Palazzo story and Morand's comments, as if the telling alone should have rendered them transparent.

That was when I saw Vanessa's face change, each word altering it a bit more, aging it, wearing on her—this appeared to me with insane clarity—like a year of disappointment and bitterness that would have made us, as a couple, moved to tenderness just moments ago by the childhood setting, into an old pair of implacable foes, while, inflamed by the idea of being this damage, this time, or whatever it might be, I continued my stupid story, in the same tone in which I would have professed my love.

Had I guessed, then, that she'd been Morand's mistress? That my insistence on repeating *Morand*, on recounting his rage at seeing me, me, in the place where they'd sat together—as if I could have known—, all the upset and disorder of which she was the cause, was infuriating her, confirming the suspicions of morbid jealousy she'd probably formed about me (and was I giving credence to them now because it would be proof of grand passion, whatever it might cost me?). Whatever the reason, I didn't stop until she burst into tears, until, in her own anger, she disowned all that she had loved, me first of all, the bastard, Morand, the practical joke named Desiderio that I'd tossed into her bed from the very first day, our unending inquisition.

Vanessa, tearfully shouting her utter disgust, lashed out that evening at everything I possessed here: the laundry, which she sent flying; the valise, which she overturned; the Desiderio manuscript, which she made as if to throw into the fire but instead tore apart as I watched, in half and in half again (was I indifferent, or did I feel that my immobility and silence were a necessary mortification?), to play the fire's part herself with infantile rage; the scarf, which she flung in my face, and which did me no harm, obviously . . .

When she stormed out, slamming the door, no sound (no voice?) escaped my lips. I stood there dazed for several minutes, staring stupidly at the knob.

There you have it. This was how, on that evening, with a few words, I ruined our last chance. I didn't even know why. I didn't even know whether I felt liberated—in which case it would have been from the farcical prospect of the life—the high life!—of a family man with two grubby children, perhaps—or unhappy. I didn't even know whether I felt any satisfaction in understanding at least the inconsequential side issues of the business: why I'd run into Vanessa C. on rue des Douves Anciennes, for example, how she could have learned details about Madame Vian's dreams from a reliable source, why Morand wanted to see me go off somewhere far away, the-devil-knows-where, and believe in the myth of Vanessa's wrongdoing when it was he, I, who were destroying her . . .

When I did finally make a move, it was to wade through the faintly tremulous sea of laundry and paper scraps, going in circles, further abasing what remained of Desiderio: pieces I had no intention of picking up. Then I noticed the money on the table and Vanessa's handbag, which she'd forgotten.

I looked at it, this bag, for a long time before touching it. (In truth, I handled it at first as if it were made of porcelain, very gingerly, breathed in its scent, and even held it to my cheek because it was burning.) Then, abruptly—as a fitting return for her childish rage: I too would smash her toys, or else to round out the desolation in the place where I'd vanquished her: it would then be over?—I opened it as wide as I could, nearly tearing its leather lips, and emptied it onto the table. I knew its contents by heart, lotions and moisturizers, cotton wool, lipstick, the address book filled with young women, the little camera, her keys. I would have readily indulged in senseless vandalism against all of it, I imagine, except that there was something else. And this something else promptly took on an inordinate importance.

It was a letter from Morand—I recognized the careful, regular hand straight away from his reply to my classified ad. But it was signed—and this was so unexpected that my aggression, transferred to a new object, took an entirely different turn, and I guffawed at the vaudevillian name: Léon! (I cried so hard with laughter that it hurt, however idiotic such a reaction may seem, as if by doing so I could take some sort of revenge on the man with the matronly wife and the grubby children, Vanessa's lover—so I thought—I was dreaming!)

What I shamelessly read thus smacked, at first, of the implausible and ridiculous. I found the declarations of love overblown. I likewise laughed at the mistakes, flaws, repetition, awkwardness, everything that made this heartfelt message a model of adolescent literature. It was only after some time had passed that I considered its content in a more serious light.

It was an interminable missive in which Morand implored Vanessa to forgive him for who-knew-what, which was the source of all their troubles—the excuses he offered were appalling—and to meet him one last time so he could explain himself in person. But, most importantly, the question at issue suddenly became one Desiderio, evidently the crime Vanessa was to pardon, to which, or to whom—Desiderio or crime—I would have given, as they say, my unbounded attention, if not for the fact that the only thing said on the subject, for pages on end, was that it, or he, would have to be forgotten one day. Forgotten!

I agonized forever over this letter without gleaning any more from it, thanks in part to my weariness and to the despondency brought on by the circumstances of Vanessa's departure, than a sense of my own blindness and that—cold comfort—of the inspector's buffoonery. With the exception, however, of the following: that the letter was dated a week ago, and that it had resulted, of this I was sure, from the bitterness Morand must have felt at seeing me order a wedding feast at his table of love—it was too funny! Also that their rendezvous was for this evening, and I persuaded myself that Vanessa, distraught, had come here first, that she'd given me a chance, her preference, in spite of everything. What good had it done me?

The address was an odd one that meant nothing to me: rue de la Limbe des Pères (Limbo of the Fathers). But I thought to myself that a lover with such a respectable reputation to uphold must have opted, in preference to the promiscuity of rue de Palaevouno, for one of the town's more secret haunts, and so, without knowing anything about it, I imagined a small, unfrequented back alley. Vanessa would perhaps be going there tonight—what about me? I was reluctant to fully embody the idiotic myth of the jealous man, playing the role all the way to the end, but this was likely my last best chance at understanding, at having done with it.

I was incensed. The reader will find it foolish that at this same time I set about marking, from force of habit or to inflict an infantile punishment on what popular novels would call my *rival*, all the errors with lipstick (or what I believed to be errors, since after rereading them ten times over I was no longer certain of anything). Later, thanks to the pigments—to the tears, even, of laughter or otherwise—that happened to be on my hands, I sullied the page still more drastically, to the point of daubing on it, in a spirit of derision, a vaguely Indian figure, which I ultimately burned along with the letter.

Could I really think of remaining, that night, with my questions and regrets, in the wasteland of that room, putting the finishing touches on whatever disaster this was with my childish tantrums?

XI

The weather outside was fine, and I was beginning to think the halcyon days were almost upon us. On the thresholds of the shops closed on Sunday, idle, smoking shopkeepers smiled at me, my face, after all this time, having doubtless become familiar. There were also bevies of young women, who would be advancing their state of undress a little further each evening until the season started, and swarms of children whose sides split as they passed me, who shouted, forgetting their dead dogs.

I hadn't put my house back in order, having had better things to do. But I'd been careful to replace everything in Vanessa's bag and was now carrying it with me, the woman's handbag making me a not altogether normal pedestrian and attracting further merriment. I hadn't unfolded the map; it was in my pocket with the rest. But I was fairly certain I wouldn't lose my way.

Once past the principal church and the bishops' residence, I turned left and left again, entering the narrow back alley I'd explored one day after telling myself it made one drop one's eyes—and I wasn't mistaken (I had some excuse for not having seen the name plaque, eaten away by rust and overgrown with ivy, which almost certainly dated to before the Revolution: its letters had become cracks in the wall itself): this was Limbe des Pères.

A little further on, in the middle of the passage, stood the shameful house that had so greatly astonished me the first time, with its Composite high fantasy overladen with scrolls and spindles, broken toothing stones at the base of the walls that would never be repaired, listing chimney pots—to be hurried past—, pediments of the type known as open, or *sans retour*.

The shutters—what was left of them—were closed, and I found the door giving onto the back alley locked, though there could hardly have been anything inside to tempt burglars. I ran my hand gently down to the bottom of the rabbet, where there were spiders and the remains of butterflies, and thought that no one had entered here for several weeks, possibly months.

Although nothing permitted me to be sure (there were no numbers along the whole length of the alley, or else they'd become invisible—I imagine no one ever searched for the address of Monsieur *** or Madame *** here, but simply knew from time immemorial), I felt certain I'd come to the place I wanted, for, in addition to the oddity of locking up what was, or was nearly, a ruin, I recalled Vanessa's face when, dragging her here and demanding of her, regarding this folly, the kind of sly, outrageous story the reader knows, she'd flung so many names at me—a face aghast, incredulous. And on that evening, I could have sworn that in doing so I'd expressed to her the most ignoble and absurd reproach imaginable, albeit unintentionally.

At the moment, there was no one inside the offending house, and scarcely had I begun to worry about looking for a refuge when a feeling as disagreeable as it was familiar came over me (I was also on the very spot where I'd thought I'd unmasked one of my pursuers, the young man from a good family with whom, later, I'd had words and a drink—given the setting, it wasn't surprising to feel, once again, the weight of watching eyes). A figure I knew well was at the end of the lane, behind my back.

The server from the Commerce was standing at the extreme edge of the terrace seating area—it encroached onto Limbe des Pères where the latter intersected the high street—smoking, making the most of the fact that this was neither the busy hour nor season. I continued toward him on my (briefly interrupted) way, and the idea struck me that here was my dreamed-of witness.

The place was empty. I bought some cigarettes and a drink. I played no game and put on no music—so that talk would be necessary. There was an honor medal on the wall (I smiled), the prize rankings of the pétanque championship, an ashtray collection many would envy. I casually mentioned the house in back. The server looked at his open hand.

"It seems it belongs to one Monsieur Morelle?" I ventured, on the off chance.

He reached with the same hand toward my shoulder, and even touched it. The back room was decorated with architecture painted on canvas.

"Someone's been telling you stories. I've never known any Morelle around here, nor anyone else for that matter."

"It does belong to someone, doesn't it?"

His open notebook swung on the end of a chain. One wanted to close it, to set it down somewhere. He moved a scallop-shaped ashtray to the left.

"Yes and no. It's been as empty as that (the ashtray) since the war. Since the previous owner died (he pouted). They say it was left to his son, or I-don't-know-what, who made his name in books up in Paris—L., do you know him?—God knows if it's true. It might be Morelle after all. No one ever sees him."

"It's a shame, being abandoned like that. I mean the house."

"Abandoned . . . Abandoned . . . yes and no."

He pushed aside yet more objects of all sorts that separated me from him on the marble counter, leaned over so as nearly to brush my cheek, took my wrist, whispered (which seemed silly for a secret that, since it implicitly accused me of blindness, I judged to be an open one) the story, a common, vulgar story, of the man who went there on certain nights, and of the lady who joined him, or the reverse—with L.'s blessing? But this was going back to the previous year.

He straightened up again to give me time to judge for myself and began wiping away the ring left by my glass. Outside, some children knocked a table as they ran. Two customers entered in their Sunday best, trading abuse over a doubtful will. I paid, and my lady's handbag drew stares.

While the server was occupied with the new arrivals inside, I took the opportunity to return to the house, impelled by the fresh inspiration that Vanessa, who often arrived first, must have a key to the place among her others. And I was not mistaken.

The door barely creaked.

The first room I saw, the one I entered, was in a state of disrepair commensurate with the frontispiece. The wood of the herringbone floor was dull and dead. Before I even knew what was what, I trod there on loose soil, water, or a fly bridge. Hanging in the air was the disagreeable odor of what I took to be moss and saltpeter.

My eyes having adjusted to the dimness, the general appearance of this probable former living room seemed nonetheless familiar, and the sensation was so intolerable (in a place with a smell that someone would think, would call *bad* in a bad book—like finding one's own thought in this bad book) that I swore at it.

It was a very naive conjuration, and I told myself that what I'd found here was simply the same general layout as the café that occupied its brother building. Except that here the billiard table, the divider of faux arcades over trompe-l'oeil vineyards, the decor of painted architecture, etc., were missing. There was no furniture, either, and the only light came from the windows facing the street—the rotted slats of the jalousies hung down, crisscrossing—the rear wall being blind.

On the other hand, boiserie panels, comb-painted and embellished with arabesques in the manner of Dugourc or Crosnier, ran all around the room, formerly adorned with mirrors (only the frame decorations remained, with a few whitish, sticky splotches in the center where one should have been able to see oneself). Behind them was sea-green pekin, faded, hanging in ribbons, on which flowering branches intertwined.

The ceiling depicted a heavenly sky—originally limpid and done in pink tones, now with clouds of grime, clouds by forfeit—so that the delicate helix staircase might well lead nowhere.

There was, nevertheless, a second-floor landing giving onto two smaller rooms, one empty and as dilapidated as downstairs (I thought, God knows why, of a guest room, it was no bigger), the other far more singular.

This was a sort of study-cum-library whose decor—I assessed it at first in the semi-darkness—, less elaborate than that of the living room (but one *knew* the living room was below, and this knowledge exuded something just as murky), seemed not to have suffered from the passage of time. There were basic furnishings as well, neither very old nor very costly, such as one might imagine belonging to a student or a young married couple on the rise: the table, the mole-skin armchair, and, in a corner, that which I had been both certain and vaguely afraid to find: the daybed. The walls were nothing but shelves filled with books, or nearly so.

This sealed-up room was stifling, and my first act was to go and open the far window, higher than that on the alley side. A jalousie and storm shutter barred access to a long-abandoned garden on the same level, which surprised me at this elevation, but which explained the disastrous dampness of the blind wall downstairs.

It must have been a terraced vegetable garden in former days, with leaves I believed I could identify as belonging to straggly tomatoes, half-wild potatoes, and tall garden angelicas among the thistles and black nightshade. There was a large tree in the center that recalled nothing to me, a pulley well with a strange mechanism. And I saw everywhere, as in those hidden-picture puzzles where you have to find the blind man's cane (it's upside-down in the foliage) or as in Easter gardens full of poorly concealed favors, incredible old things, shards, disemboweled chairs, taken over by amaryllises and poppies.

I couldn't see to the end of it, but clearly what I had here was the last remaining scrap of the parceled-up manor grounds, of which the two follies formed the entrance and the bishops' residence the main house. It crossed my mind that Vanessa, escaping my surveillance on that first evening through the lapidary museum, had done no more than cut across to this place.

I left the French door ajar to contemplate the study in the daylight. I was proven to have had the right of it over the server, in that this room, at least, must have received daily maintenance. The parquet floor and furniture smelled of wax. I could draw a finger across the spines or glazed backs of the books (these, and the objects on the table—a typewriter, a lamp, pens, paper, even flowers—attested that love was not the only activity taking place here) and there wasn't a particle of dust. There were no traces of rising damp on the ceiling, which was white.

The reader may smile at the fact that, without even realizing it, I was caressing the shelves in this way, but also: I stretched out full length on the bed, I ran my fingers over the typewriter keys—one would have thought I was about to play something—I plugged in the desk lamp—it worked—and unplugged it, I sat in the moleskin armchair.

Neither Vanessa nor Morand was on time for their rendezvous, but I could see reasons for this. Vanessa could have little to expect from the explanations promised by her former lover, nor especially from the desperate pleas he would surely make to her—so I thought—since nothing could ever start over again and be as it had been before, either for him or for me. Had she intended to come nonetheless, she would have had to make a detour to rue de Nazareth, if for no other reason than to collect the handbag, the keys, the papers.

As for Morand, I wondered how someone might manage to deliver himself from his family on a Sunday and imagined his lies. Would he even try to break free, when it came to that? It seemed to me, on the contrary, though nothing, with the exception of his tardiness, corroborated this conviction, that he would abandon the idea at the last moment—out of courage, incidentally, or out of weakness? I wondered, too, how he'd been able to secure the use of a house that its owner still haunted. Was L. aware of the inspector's amorous adventures?—and for the first time I looked at the bed with a feeling of intractable pain, so much sickening salaciousness did I ascribe to the man, to the point that this futile, stupid question gradually supplanted all the others: Could he close his eyes to this?

Until another sense of unease, even more insidious, more unmasterable—doubtless because everything screamed "trap" in this immaculate scene, where, in the absence of Morand, who was to meet whom?—convinced me of this self-evident fact, a dizzying one: *Why, indeed, would Morand come at all, since I was there, I who had never ceased to search, to love, to torture in his stead?*

It was to escape the still-unanswered questions, and chimeras such as these, as much as to steady my nerves, that I turned my attention to the books on the shelves. It was only then that I made the most bizarre discovery this troublesome house held in store for me.

I'd taken down a book at random, then two, then at least ten, and in every case it was a novel by L. The master of the house was not unknown to me: I must have read two or three of his works, but I hadn't known he'd published more, let alone enough to cover the walls of an entire room.

Yet I soon found, in the midst of the thousand volumes he attributed to himself, one title (the first was *Theory of Gardens* in two volumes, which I knew to be by a forgotten eighteenth-century architect for having read it, long ago, with passionate interest), then a hundred more, among them the most blatantly well known, which loudly proclaimed the deception, a puerile one when all was said and done.

Doubtless this costly and presumptuous fantasy by which L. had appropriated the masterpieces of Alexandre Dumas *père* and Jules Verne, among others—I've forgotten most of them—would have elicited a smile had not my impatience brought me to the point of exasperation instead, and had not one volume, which promised to be more personal, soon aroused my curiosity.

I sat down again at the desk and had begun to read the insert when I became aware of a presence in the house.

The door at which I was staring, with its handsome porcelainlike knob, opened, while, even before seeing her, as if the weight of the past, my regrets or whatever they might have been, imprinted on the slowness of the movement something immediately recognizable: her tiredness, perhaps, liberated from her body, I knew it to be Vanessa.

Never before had she seemed so beautiful, with the regular oval of her face, the fineness of her straight nose, the very white line dividing her hair which she'd done up in a knot in back, *en couronne*.

Also makeup which seemed extraordinary because, deprived of her usual stock, which was nature itself to me, she must have supplied the deficiency in some other way. She'd also changed her clothes, and wore a white bodice with flutter sleeves, low cut, already a summer dress.

She showed no surprise at seeing me in the other's place. I would say: on the contrary, if that movement of the hands really was like one of my mother's when she would hold me back on the verge of an intrepid expedition—she saying *little Columbus, little Ader*—the manifestly futile conjuration against a foreseeable risk: I was going to go anyway. She was merely sad.

Stepping through the doorframe, she approached the desk, where I was at a loss for words. I handed her the bag, but it was only to do something that would be a prelude, according to my way of thinking, to an explanation at last. Then she would have said yes or no and we would have continued on interminably, with a clear understanding.

But Vanessa simply said a very soft *thank you*—which was neither yes thank you nor no thank you: a purely perfunctory speech act, which devastated me—while, before even giving me time to collect myself (was it to show me that she was henceforth free? or to defend herself against an attachment she still felt? I wanted to believe as much), she turned toward the French door, which I myself had left open to escapes of all kinds, and disappeared into the garden.

I must have flung, in a very silly and instinctive manner, my hands out toward her, to warn her, if nothing else, that there were nettles outside she'd need to step over, furniture with splinters, nails, glass, that to flee that way was folly. But with the table and armchair holding me prisoner, the pages taking flight in the outdraft

JEAN LAHOUGUE

(stupidly, I tried to catch them), the typewriter, the lamp, the vase I nearly knocked over, constituting so many monstrous obstacles in my path—I was blundering into everything—I made it to the terrace far too late to catch her and make her stay.

The garden was as before, and I searched in vain for the path she had forged, to the bishops' residence in all likelihood, so completely had the weeds of all descriptions closed up again behind her. How long did I stay there like that, hands dangling at my sides and empty, empty, never ceasing to betray the absence of a lady's handbag, like that of any other toy snatched away by surprise, calling after her?

I stayed a long time, too, at the table, listless, my face in my hands, obsessed by the clownish thought that I had to see L. by any means possible, that he'd given his blessing to Morand and Vanessa's little arrangement and was going to know to what other monstrous intrigues he was leaving his door open.

I'd even taken a sheet of paper and begun to write *Sir, Dear Sir, Dear Friend*, etc., successively crossed out, and a draft of a letter that was impossible because I was going around in circles, because my questions quickly became of an informulable indiscretion, because I was accumulating, as with the letter to Vanessa, inexplicable awkwardnesses behind which my feelings and interests in the matter showed through plain as day.

It seemed to me that I wouldn't be able to speak this evening about anything but me and her, and that I needed to begin at the beginning: the day when, crossing the wrong way through the Utopias' reception area, I'd thought she belonged to the place. Then there'd been the classified ad and the evening on rue des Douves Anciennes, the Palazzo, my doubts, and the sea—I thought that talking about it, making something of it, would deliver me. As if drawing up an inventory of what I knew about Vanessa C.—but one always knows more—could have served to conjure it away.

And so I placed, almost unthinkingly, a sheet of paper in the roller, and typed the story as it came to me, having just enough good sense to omit the names, to switch locations and events when they would have implicated some person or other, without order, without taste, without remorse or pentimenti.

However fragmented this portrait of Vanessa, owing to this probably detestable automatic writing, I persuaded myself that it would be clear to anyone who'd known her or had been involved with the preceding events, either directly or indirectly, as when someone says *face* and the image arises of this particular face and it alone. I even reasoned, after a fashion, that my naivetes—and God knows I must have let some through, writing the way one loves—would take such a turn that they could have been caused by Vanessa C.'s nudity and none other, that, behind the impotence, the body would be recognized.

When I'd finished the work, or rather when it had so exhausted me that a single word more would have been painful and a lie, I'd covered some twenty pages I did not even dare reread, for fear I should have to tear them up.

This hastily dashed-off effort, the shame at having had to ask the questions it raised, and the care I'd taken in spite of it all to disguise people and places, tempted me to withhold my own name. And yet, the vague hope I entertained of obtaining a reply compelled me to furnish an address (it was ready to hand: rue de

Nazareth would not betray me anytime soon) and a nondescript surname.

I immediately thought of Desiderio because of L. himself, who'd set me the example by taking credit for the books he loved— perhaps he'd see this as an additional mark of recognition and gratitude. Also, I suppose, because I'd always felt a need for the *tombeau* already described—and it was for its paradoxically Desiderian title that I'd chosen this book by L. from among the others a little while ago: *Vacated Landscape*, from which Vanessa had torn me . . .

To make doubly sure, I also gave Lievel as a reference in a short cover letter, as someone who knew both too much and too little about the origins of my actions, and whom L. knew well, having taken credit for all his books. Would he venture to go and resurrect the old writer who had sunk into the world's indifference? And what unsparing portrait would the other paint of me? It was of no importance.

Then I used everything I could find in the cardboard boxes to make up a suitable parcel and quit the house.

Outside it was nighttime, or nearly so, something I'd barely noticed while upstairs, my eyes, in order to write, having adjusted to the obscurity. Someone I took for a drunk was standing in the shadows at the corner of the house—possibly one of the café customers from earlier. His eyes followed me insistently.

As it happened, I stopped in at the café, which was still open. Other customers were finishing their meals amid the sounds of knives and glasses. I felt, at the sight of them, and because I hadn't eaten in ten hours, a pain in the pit of my stomach—but I no longer had enough money. All I bought were stamps for my parcel. The server was busy adding up several interminable bills at the same time and paid no attention to me whatever.

I went through the center of town, where the illumination on the facades was still absurd, given the pale sky: there were no shadows. It seemed as if someone might punch through the thin surface with his hand and at once be behind it. In the fountain square a lady was crumbling bread that didn't fall but instead took wind, blew between my legs. Everywhere knives and glasses could be heard.

I walked to the main post office, which, for its part, was dark, and felt along the wall to the letterbox, in reality a narrow opening. My parcel had every defect including that of being an embarrassment to me, but it was slender and slipped through to the other side. At the *** Press they would forward it to L.

I next turned my steps toward rue de Nazareth, having nothing more to do—so I believed—but wait, and get some sleep if I could. I turned my steps, but all sorts of vertiginous thoughts cast my mind anxiously back to rue de la Limbe des Pères, beginning with the prospect of returning to my landlady's house, the old woman—who glorified her dead son, building chimerical sanctuaries for him that bore such a strong resemblance to L.'s madness that I could just as easily have dreamed the end of her dream, reality itself—, so old, I thought, that she would soon die. Passing through my pursuers, whom the silhouette from a short while before had brought to mind again (in that instance, sooner than the young man, I would have envisioned the imaginary witnesses to that which separated my unfortunate attempts from my projected plan, in an impossible space, but to save myself from what?). And

JEAN LAHOUGUE

my bare hands that I was deliberately planing along the walls of V., and to which the idea of an evening without loving—I thought to myself too, but it may have been naivete: without theater—recalled the book that I'd forgotten.

But I suppose the house itself had never ceased to attract me, which was unjustifiable with its living room leagues under the sea, its one bedroom empty and the other not, with, too, its unexpected garden that one wanted to reclaim because it would constitute a charming retreat on sunny days, but that one wouldn't touch, however, because it was perhaps nothing more than its abandonment—one would never be but on the verge.

Arrived at the intersection, just before home, feeling I was guilty of an evasion, I abruptly turned around and headed back. What else could I do?

In front of the folly, the silhouette—or its relief, male or female— was still at its post. I felt a fleeting temptation to go over and ask them something, but the idea that I would find drunken flesh or ill will dissuaded me. In truth, the figure was, in the night now altogether black—with no sound or halo of lamplight to indicate any soul remained at the Commerce—, much more disquieting than pitiable. I wanted to lock the door behind me but, to my misfortune, I must have put the key back in Vanessa's bag, and slamming the worm-eaten panel or doing nothing at all amounted to the same thing.

I recrossed the pekin living room in slightly ridiculous fashion, by the glow of a lighter that illuminated nothing but my hand.

Then I reached the library where I lit, not without relief, the table lamp.

I went to close the French door, owing to the moths and numerous insects that thought themselves in the sunshine, on the garden—it could no longer be seen. Then I settled myself on the other side of the room with the book.

I opened it, not to the beginning, but, as was my quasi-professional and rather annoying habit, to the final pages, where the narrator, having once, through lack of courage, signed himself Desiderio—here I smiled—was reduced to a fictional character, at best a historical one. At which point the author suddenly and nonchalantly shifted from *I* to *you* and from past tense to present, and it was then that I read (scarcely, amid the turmoil into which they plunged me, did I hear the door below slam shut behind my pursuer, no doubt, and his hesitant step on the stair) these strange words:

It is high time you called off your dogs, you, the woman or old man who has always been running in my shadow. This hunt does not lead to much. Mount again the few steps that separate you from my final refuge, it is light there at last. Open the door, it is only pushed to, I am no longer making love. All you need do is close this book before me, before you, beneath the lamp, for me to disappear—and this will be justice—within your indifference as at the bottom of the sea. Then look at the time on your wrist, it will forever be that of my death.

TRANSLATOR'S AFTERWORD

Jean Lahougue, best known for his post–*nouveau roman* novels that often incorporate sophisticated word games, oulipian constraints, and innovative metatextual techniques, grew up reading golden-age mystery writers like Agatha Christie and Georges Simenon, an enthusiasm that has never dimmed. Detective fiction in general, and these two authors in particular, permeate much of his work. *Comptine des Height*, which won the Prix Médicis in 1980 (the prize went to Jean-Luc Benoziglio after Lahougue refused it), is set at an English country house isolated by a snowstorm over the Christmas holidays, during which time ten inmates are murdered one by one in an echo of Christie's *Ten Little Indians*. *La Doublure de Magrite* follows a young actor named Magrite (an anagram of the famous Maigret) as he plays a character called "Inspector Magrite" in an amateur theater production and later witnesses a real crime. Lahougue uses a variety of techniques to subvert, pastiche, rewrite, deconstruct, and transform his sources, repurposing them in order to examine how we read books and how books read each other. *Vacated Landscape* can be grouped in with these detective-themed novels, but it stands a little apart in that its metatextual and postmodern elements, though still present throughout, remain inconspicuous—there to be found, but subtle enough to be overlooked—until the revelatory final page. Rather than proclaiming a direct relation to a specific mystery writer's work, the novel draws on generic tropes: a letter from a stranger, a disappearance, an amateur sleuth, a skeptical police inspector, an alluring woman with a hidden past. And even these connections are downplayed in the opening chapters, which do not particularly evoke the genre, much less give overt signals that metatextual games are being played with it. If anything, their tone suggests a grown-up version of the boys' adventure stories the narrator edits. At first blush, then, the book seems to wear its literary influences lightly. It is, in fact, one of those rare finds, a novel that that can be as simple or as complex as the reader wants it to be.

The special affinity the *nouveau roman* and its later offshoots has for detective fiction has been well documented, as has Jean Lahougue's membership in this tradition,[1] though *Landscape* has received less critical attention than his other novels, perhaps for the reasons noted above. The genre lends itself well to the sorts of experiments that interest novelists of these schools because mystery writers were doing many of these same experiments for mainstream audiences long before the *nouveau roman* or postmodernism existed. They share a common fondness for clues and games, for formal constraints (think of Agatha Christie's novels in which the murders are patterned on a particular nursery rhyme), incomplete or conflicting narratives, self-conscious exploration of the process of "reading" a set of facts to construct a meaning, and enlisting the reader's active participation in this process, to name just a few. Lahougue's work engages with all of this and adds a special emphasis on a few trademark preoccupations and writing strategies.

One notable example is the mise en abyme. *Vacated Landscape* teems with them, though in typical Lahougue fashion, all are partial, doubtful, qualified, or distorted. The most obvious are the Desiderio manuscript and, later, the narrator's own manuscript. The circumstances surrounding their production appear to have been the same, but we can only guess at how similar they are in substance, since we have to rely on abbreviated summaries that deal more with atmosphere than specifics. We sense, however, that the two texts must be closely related: fraternal twins, if not identical. They may, in fact, be triplets, if we include the handwritten draft poor Sergeant L. spends his free time piecing together behind the scenes. Is *Vacated Landscape* itself coextensive with any or all of these? At about twenty pages each, their length would seem to preclude the idea, but the novel's style and content argue strongly and persistently in favor of its being the narrator's manuscript. The novel's sentences hem and haw, interrupt themselves with dashes and parentheticals, and occasionally delay the reader's understanding until the very end, requiring some to be read more than once in order to parse them. They abound in dependent clauses, produced by artfully placed commas (doubly artful because they have to masquerade as *carelessly* placed commas) whose relation to each other is often unclear at first, creating further ambiguity where there would otherwise be none. Even some simple nouns have an oddly provisional feel: there is the eating establishment that vacillates between being a bar, a café, and a bar-café before eventually settling into its proper name, and the window (*fenêtre*) transformed in a subsequent paragraph into a French door (*porte-fenêtre*). The narrator seems to be aware of the confusion he might be causing and often feels the need to explain himself ("what I mean is . . ."). To preserve this hasty, first-draft quality, I have kept in two orphaned parentheses that may or may not have been typos, as well as the misspelled names of a few historical figures: De Nome, Thierry, Kije, and de Dominici. If we trust to this evidence and accept that a twenty-page pamphlet, by some act of transubstantiation, can become the body of the novel in condensed, concentrated form, then this would place us, rather ominously, at the end of the chain of transmission in which Morelle and the narrator are also links. The frequent interpolation of phrases such as *already known to the reader*, *the aforementioned*, and *described above* are further evidence for this hypothesis, and at the same time subtle reminders that what's being said has been said before, that even first-time readers are in fact already *re*reading. The irony is that, in a book where rereading and rewriting are so crucial, and are foregrounded in diverse ways both large and small, these manuscripts (at least the narrator's) have had the benefit of neither.

The cities in the Utopias Museum are possible mises en abyme as well. Such cities are presented as semiotic spaces, texts written in the language of brick and stone, meant to be read rather than inhabited. That the town of V. in *Landscape* also functions as a semiotic space is, I think, part (but only part) of the reason for the book's preoccupation with walls, doors, windows, and facades—and, of course, with the utopian cities themselves, which are described so as to imply parallels between designing these cities and writing fiction. It is significant that the work of Monsu Desiderio, the painter of architectural landscapes the narrator so admires, is included in the same collection. Significant, too, that his paintings, though theoretically present, are in actuality absent from the museum, replaced by smaller-than-life facsimiles of themselves. For all these potential representations of the novel, we have only spotty second-hand descriptions, and must connect the dots ourselves, much like the narrator does with the pointillist outline he plots of Jean Morelle's route through town.

Lahougue's novel contains nothing that is not a motif. Select any element and you'll find it reproduced fractally at different scales: the winding progress of the narrator's investigative journey is mirrored in miniature by the reader's progress through the sentences, for example, and through the book as a whole; it is also mirrored in the physical geography of V., a town one feels must be spiral-shaped like the narrator's seashells and the local ammonites, or at least arranged in some way that defies the logic of rectilinear grids ("I believed the roads straight," the narrator says, "but they bent imperceptibly"). Each of these ideas functions as a metaphor for the others, giving nearly every passage in the book a double or triple meaning, though none is identifiable as the tenor, or ultimate referent, of these metaphors. Instead, the various metaphorical vehicles are like a series of arrows arranged in a ring, each pointing to the next. Circularity, repetition, and doubling are evident from the macro level to the micro, right down to individual words. Certain key terms like *desire*, *justify*, *chance*, *dream*, *naive*, *in truth*, and *vague* (among a host of others) gradually insinuate themselves into the reader's awareness through their frequent recurrence. Other words create their own echoes through polyvalence, with secondary meanings that cluster around a few discernible themes to form networks running perpendicular to the words' primary meanings, like a warp through a weft—religion, law, and theater being among the most prominent.

The absent Morelle, object of the narrator's search, forms the central node of a special network all his own that illustrates Lahougue's virtuosity at these word games—another trademark feature of his fiction. Hopscotch is *la marelle* in French, and *morelles* are plants in the nightshade family, including, most notably, *Atropa belladonna*. There is even an item that might be interpreted as a *mérelle*—the scallop shell that is a traditional symbol of the Camino de Santiago, the pilgrimage made along the Way of St. James. This is in addition to the near namesakes it immediately calls to mind, such as *The Invention of Morel* and Charles Morel in *The Remembrance of Things Past*. Each of these nodes fits lock-and-key into larger patterns of meaning within the book, for all the world as if they were expressly designed for this purpose instead of strewn throughout the language by the random hand of etymological chance. Another Easter-egg namesake, which I will spoil for readers only because I can find no record of an English translation by which they might uncover it on their own, comes from Luc-Vincent Thiéry's 1787 guidebook, *Guide des amateurs et des étrangers voyageurs à Paris: ou description raisonnée de cette ville, de sa banlieue, et de tout ce qu'elles contiennent de remarquable* (Guide to Paris for enthusiasts and foreign travelers, or an annotated description of the city, her suburbs, and everything of note they contain). The two folly houses near the end of *Vacated Landscape*, along with their decor and rear garden, have been lifted intact from volume one of this work, though the narrator seems not to recognize them. If he had, he might have recalled that Thiéry tosses in the architect's surname at the end of his description, almost as an afterthought: Morel.

This is just one of the multifarious ways Lahougue makes use of other texts in his novels, according to procedures that vary from book to book but that always involve multiple source texts and multiple modes of transformation, from oblique allusions to direct quotations. The aim is more radical and more ambitious than simple commentary. Like L., the absentee owner of the folly house, he claims these books as his own; he rewrites them retroactively without changing a word, something akin to the way Borges says every author creates his own precursors. Jean-Marie Morel (the Easter eggs keep coming), the author of *Theory of Gardens*, another eighteenth-century book that gets a brief mention in the final chapter, advocated a more natural style of design that embraced local terrain rather than forcing nature into angular geometric forms, and thought curved pathways more appealing than rigidly straight, symmetrical ones. After reading *Landscape*, it is hard not to see this and other sections of his horticultural treatise as a meditation on narrative, one of the many frameworks for thinking about literature Lahougue tucks into his novel. Speaking of stark demarcations at the boundaries of walled-in properties and the practice of softening these by fitting them with gate openings or substituting ha-has, Morel says: "This crude finishing never deceives, but its invention proves that all obvious enclosures are displeasing, because it always produces a secret uneasiness that leads to a desire to broach these limits . . ." Words to be kept in mind when following the narrator in his descent from the Heaven of gloriously incomplete texts into the fallen world of enclosures and crude finishings.

NOTE

1. For an in-depth exploration of this relationship, see *Detecting Texts: The Metaphysical Detective Story from Poe to Postmodernism*, edited by Patricia Merivale and Susan Elizabeth Sweeney, which includes a discussion of Lahougue in Michel Sirvent's essay, "Reader-Investigators in the Post-*Nouveau Roman*: Lahougue, Peeters, and Perec."

K. E. Gormley (1978–) is an American translator living near Philadelphia.